Ribbon on the Willow

Ribbon on the Willow
Copyright © 2020 by Jody Cleven

All rights reserved. No part of this publication may be reproduced, distributed, or transmitted in any form or by any means, including photocopying, recording, or other electronic or mechanical methods, without the prior written permission of the publisher, except in the case of brief quotations embodied in critical reviews and certain other noncommercial uses permitted by copyright law. Permission requests should be sent to info@writewaypublishingcompany.com.
Printed in the United States of America

ISBN 978-1-946425-70-6 Softcover

Book Design by CSinclaire Write-Design
Book Cover Design by James Hislope

• Other Books •

A Ripple in Maggie Pond

• Coming Soon •

*Red Shed Books:
The Annex*

For Randy.

Every Princess needs a Prince.

Ribbon
on the
Willow

Jody Cleven

• BARNSLEY INK •
RALEIGH, NORTH CAROLINA

CONTENTS

Willodean 1
The Party. 5
Panic. 9
Gone, But Not Forgotten 13
The White Ribbon 19
Unless You're Dead or Dying 24
Fun, Food, and Fellowship 29
Dunk or Be Dunked 34
Yolk's on You 43
Mittens and Boots 49
Close Call 56
The Munch Bunch. 61
Grazie, Signora Winters 67
Thirteen Red Ribbons. 77
Love-All 83
Bluebirds of Happiness 85
TK. 89
Badminton, Anyone? 93
Rudy 101
Help 106
Willodean Adorned Again 113
Norman 120
Home for Christmas 123
Silent Night, Holy Night 130

The Quad 134
Sweet Release 138
Goodbye Birdie. 141
A Plan Takes Shape 144
A Better Benton 146
What Would it Take?. 153
Lake Side. 156
The News Spreads 161
As Luck Would Have It. 163
A Storm Approaches 167
Hold on Tight. 174
Cleanup. 178
Birdie Craze 183
Something Very Special to Celebrate 189

CHAPTER ONE

Willodean

SPENCER WILSON HAD WALKED by the willow tree in his front yard more times than he could count. It had been there his entire life. When he walked past it on this day, he smiled when he saw the red ribbon. Twelve. That's what the ribbon meant today. Spencer grew up in his small Southern town known only for tobacco fields, hurricane warnings, sweet tea, and seven churches. Spencer lived in his house on Cardinal Lane with his parents, grandfather, siblings, and his cat and dog. His mom was a teacher at the local elementary school. She had been his second grade teacher and had taught most of his friends too. Among the teachers at Benton Elementary, she was one of the favorites.

Spencer's best friend, Claire Champion, lived directly across the street in their cul-de-sac neighborhood that was dotted with crepe myrtles and dogwood trees. Claire and Spencer had been friends since daycare. She shared his interest in fishing, hiking, and nature in general, so they were a great match. Claire embraced her title of neighborhood tomboy. She felt more comfortable in a pair of black high-top tennis shoes and a worn sweatshirt than fancy sandals and a Sunday dress.

Claire knew what this particular red ribbon on the willow meant when she spied it from her second floor bedroom window that February morning as she was getting ready for school. A tinge of excitement came over her when she saw the ribbon tails fluttering in the morning breeze. She smiled a satisfied smile when she looked at the box by her bedside table. The box was secured with a red ribbon of its own. "It's perfect," she said to herself. She believed it was time for an upgrade, and that's why she'd spent the better part of four months' allowance on this birthday present. She could hardly wait until the party this evening to see if Spencer agreed.

Most of the families in Spencer and Claire's neighborhood had come to expect a red ribbon making a periodic appearance on the tree in the Wilson's front yard. Some knew the tradition behind the ribbons, others did not. Claire's friend Jessica had moved into the neighborhood just a month earlier, so it was the first time she'd seen a ribbon on the tree. While the two girls were waiting for the other neighborhood kids to arrive at the morning bus stop, Jessica pointed to the tree in Spencer's yard and asked, "What's with that ribbon?"

"Ah," Claire responded, "you'll see those ribbons throughout the year. Whenever anything special happens in the Wilson family—like a birthday, a perfect report card for one of the kids, or a job promotion for one of the parents—a ribbon gets tied around the tree. This one is for Spencer's birthday."

"That's really cool," Jess said. "So, they've been doing that for a long time?"

"For as far back as I can remember."

Just then Spencer walked up and joined the girls on the corner. "Happy birthday, Spencer!" Jess said.

"Oh, thanks. You saw the ribbon?"

"Yeah, Claire was just telling me about the ribbon tradition. That's really cool. Is it always red?"

"Yep," Spencer said, "it's red because of a tradition that my dad grew up with from the time he was a little boy. When anyone in the family was having a special day, Grandma Wilson would set a special red plate at their place at the dinner table. When Mom married Dad, she decided to continue the tradition but use a red ribbon instead of a plate.

So, yeah. It's always red. Well, except for three times. The only time the ribbon changed colors was when a Wilson baby was born. A pink ribbon was tied around Willodean when my sister, Abby, came home from the hospital and blue ribbons for when me and my little brother, Rudy, were born."

"Willodean?" Jess asked. "The tree has a name?"

"Yeah, we call the tree Willodean named after my great-grandmother who started the red plate tradition. Since the tree was a willow, it seemed to fit."

Looking over at the ribbon Claire had to agree. It was a pretty cool tradition. For the thirteenth time, Spencer's birthday ribbon was tied neatly around Willodean. The tradition lived on.

CHAPTER TWO

The Party

EVER SINCE SPENCER COULD remember, his mom had made him a special birthday cake. Actually, it was cake and ice cream together, so the perfect combination. Cake-cream is what the Wilson kids called it. How his mom did it was a mystery to him, but Spencer loved the pinwheel design that the rich chocolate cake and creamy white ice cream made as they swirled together to form the cake-cream. The twelve candles that sat atop the chocolate and ice cream cylinder were bright red, just like the ribbon tied around Willodean's trunk.

Besides Spencer's family, the only other party guest was Claire. While Mrs. Wilson was in the kitchen pouring fizzy soft drinks into plastic cups,

Spencer's dad arrived with three large, flat boxes. The familiar scent of pizza mixed with warm cardboard that always seems to accompany takeout pizza immediately filled the Wilson living room.

"Pizza's here," Mr. Wilson called out as the kids trailed him into the kitchen.

After the group had their fill of pepperoni pizza and soda, they gathered around the cake-cream while Mrs. Wilson lit the twelve red candles. Led by Claire, who loved to sing, everyone broke into a robust rendition of "Happy Birthday" while Spencer watched them with a contended grin.

When it came time for presents, Spencer reached first for the large box that Claire had lugged over that afternoon. "Claire, what in the world did you did get me?" he asked as he yanked the red ribbon off the box and tore at the wrapping.

"Oh cool!" Spencer exclaimed when he saw the pro badminton set she'd bought him. "We needed this!" He scanned the large box that held the net, rackets, and birdies.

Spencer and Claire had been playing badminton since his parents had gotten him a junior badminton set when he turned eight years old. It was the same year that Claire (with permission from Spencer's parents) had given him a smoky gray kitten with a black-tipped tail.

The kids and the cat enjoyed badminton from the start. Spencer and Claire caught on to the game immediately and both seemed to have a natural knack for it. The cat eyed the birdie going back and forth over the net. It was what earned him his name "Birdie." Those days, back when Spencer and Claire were eight years old, were the first of many days that the two would spend playing badminton together.

Spencer turned over the box of his pro badminton set—the third set Spencer had owned—and looked forward to getting the new net set up. Birdie nudged Spencer's leg as to say, *If you're not going to open the rest of those presents, I will.* Spencer patted Birdie on the head and grabbed another present off the top of the stack.

Spencer's parents gave him a new fishing pole, tackle, and a several accessories for his electronics. Grandpa Theodore gave him a pair of polarized sunglasses to use while out at the creek fishing. Abby, who was three years older than Spencer and had her own babysitting money, bought him a set of artist colored pencils that he'd seen at the craft store in town. Rudy, who was six and had no money of his own, made Spencer a card with a picture of a cat and a bird on it. It was a great birthday all around.

After all the presents had been opened, Grandpa Theodore and Mrs. Wilson cleaned up the birthday party mess from the living room and the kitchen. Grandpa had moved in with Spencer's family after Grandma Wilson died almost three years earlier. He considered the help he gave his daughter-in-law with the dishes and household chores his rent money. Truth be told, it kept him young, so his son and daughter-in-law were happy to let him help. After washing the dishes and discarding all the wrapping paper, the adults sat at the kitchen table drinking coffee, Rudy disappeared into the den to watch a video, and Abby retired to her room upstairs to text her friends.

Since it was unusually warm for mid-February, Spencer and Claire headed out to the backyard to set up the badminton net. They were amazed at how the new, upgraded rackets added a level of precision to their already competitive game. The friends played until the evening sun hung low in the cloudless Carolina sky. As always, faithful Birdie watched the two volley the lightweight cone back and forth as if they were batting away all their troubles.

Spencer's parents and Grandpa Theodore watched from the kitchen window as the two played.

"He's growing up fast, Megan," Grandpa Theodore said to Mrs. Wilson.

"I know," she responded. "Won't be long before we're carryin' him off to college."

"Not so fast, you two," Spencer's dad said. "Let him at least enjoy his carefree middle school days."

But little did they know, the days ahead would not be carefree for Spencer Wilson. In fact, troubles were right around the corner.

CHAPTER THREE

Panic

MRS. WILSON ALWAYS MADE her family pancakes for breakfast on Saturday mornings. The Saturday after Spencer's twelfth birthday was no different. As she was cleaning up after breakfast, she heard Spencer yell, "Mom, can you help me please?" The panic in Spencer's voice brought Mrs. Wilson running from the kitchen.

"What is it, sweetheart?" Spencer's mom asked as she spotted Spencer frantically looking under the couch with the aid of the flashlight on his phone. "What on earth are you looking for?"

"Birdie. I can't find him anywhere! Have you seen him?"

"What's all the commotion?" asked Grandpa Theodore as he entered the living room with

Spencer's dad trailing behind. By this time, Abby had come out of her room and was standing on the balcony overlooking the living room below. Even Max, the family's Golden Retriever, came trotting in, sensing an emergency.

"Birdie's missing," said Mrs. Wilson calmly, "but let's not panic just yet. He's got to be around here somewhere."

An all-out cat hunt turned up nothing after an exhausting forty-five minute search of the Wilson house, the yard, and the area around the front sidewalk. Spencer even called Claire to see if Birdie had wandered over to her house to investigate the scenery across the street. No luck. All that did was add one more to the search party.

Claire quickly made her way across the street to join Spencer and his family as they looked under dressers, through trash cans, inside cabinets, and behind chair cushions. Every nook and cranny was searched for a missing cat. Each closet was turned inside out. Places searched by one family member were searched again by another. Everyone started searching irrationally in places much too tiny for the cat to hide—like thin center desk drawers, small pocketbooks, and even the cookie jar.

Spencer became more distraught with each passing minute. Even the normally calm and unruffled Grandpa Theodore wore a look of worry. That cat had been in the family since Spencer was eight. It was impossible to think Birdie had simply vanished. But, as many cat owners learn the hard way, sometimes cats just wander off. Sadly, that's what appeared to have happened to Birdie Wilson. Vanished, without a trace.

The search party's focused mission was interrupted by a shout from Mrs. Wilson. "I know!" she said with a smile of relief. "Before I started the dishes, I took Spencer's old badminton set and some other toys up to the attic to save for the community tag sale. I'll bet Birdie followed me up there and got shut in."

Spencer led the way as the others followed his mad dash toward the walk-up attic stairs. Spencer reached the stairs before the others caught up to him and flung open the door. No Birdie. As quickly as relief had come over the search party thinking the mystery was solved, their hopes were dashed. After repeated searches of the attic, the seven searchers descended without a cat.

"I was *sure* that was it," Mrs. Wilson said as sweat dripped from her flushed face. A small tear left a track in the dust on Spencer's face. Nothing anyone said could console the boy who feared the worst for his faithful feline friend. Nothing.

"Spencer," Dad said gently, "he's been gone just a few hours. Surely he'll turn up by tonight. If not, we'll widen our search tomorrow."

But tomorrow came and went without any sign of Birdie. Days missing turned into weeks, and weeks into months. No one could remember when they officially stopped looking. Months after the disappearance of Birdie, Spencer's mom would catch herself looking under the beds or behind the laundry hamper for the missing cat, knowing all the while the sheer unlikeliness of him being there. Every so often Spencer and Claire would meet on the bench under the shade of Willodean and, using the set of artist pencils Abby gave him for his birthday, make fresh posters to tack on the tall Carolina pines that dotted their quiet neighborhood.

**MISSING: GRAY CAT.
GOES BY THE NAME BIRDIE.
IF FOUND, CONTACT
SPENCER WILSON—REWARD!!!**

But for all the searching and the **MISSING** posters, the disappearance of Spencer's beloved cat remained a mystery. When Spencer accepted that Birdie would never be found, he asked his mom if he could get another cat. She said that Max was pet enough and so that's how it stayed. Max was getting older, and Spencer agreed that it would be best for the Wilsons to focus their attention on their faithful Golden. After that, Birdie was mentioned less and less frequently around the Wilson household.

CHAPTER FOUR

Gone, But Not Forgotten

SPENCER ALWAYS JOKED THAT if he had a nickel for every time he heard his mom say how quickly the days and months seemed to fly by, he'd be the richest kid on the block. He usually didn't agree with her on that sentiment, but he had to admit sixth grade seemed to be flying by. It had been almost three months since his birthday and since the disappearance of Birdie.

"How can it be time for you to go on the sixth grade spring zoo trip already, Spence?" Mrs. Wilson asked her son over breakfast that morning.

"I don't know, Mom, but I'm glad you mentioned the field trip. I need to return my permission slip today. And I need extra money to go into the traveling exhibit *Fantastic Breeds of Domesticated Cats*. I'd really like to see that!"

"Sure," Mrs. Wilson said and then added, "I hope you have fun! I remember *my* sixth grade zoo trip when I was at Benton. No special cat exhibit, but it did rain cats—and dogs—the whole day!" Mrs. Wilson laughed at her own joke.

Spencer just shook his head and thought how strange it was that his mom went down the same path he was going down when she was a sixth grader so many years ago. Benton Middle School hadn't changed much over the years.

Since it was such a small school, the kids at BMS remained in one classroom with a homeroom teacher who taught all their subjects except art, music, and physical education. And as far back as anyone could remember, the sixth grade class at Benton Middle School went to the zoo for their spring field trip. It was sort of a rite of passage for BMS kids as they finished their first year of middle school. In fact, a standing joke among teachers centered around *leaving* a few students there after visiting. It was just too good of a zinger. They simply couldn't pass it up.

"I hope we're in the same group on the field trip," Claire said to Spencer as they rode the bus to school that morning.

"Me too," said Spencer, "but I heard that Ms. Jasper is dividing the chaperone teams into all-boy and all-girl groups."

Claire said, "Okay, we'll see. If she does, we can catch up later."

Although Claire and Spencer spent much of their time together, they both had other friends too. Spencer and his friends rode skateboards at the outdoor skate park or played video games. While Claire liked to skateboard, she also liked to go to the mall with her friends and shop for nothing at all, just hang around the food court watching people, talking about kids from school, and speculating who the next new couple would be at Benton Middle School.

Her friends were a little jealous of her relationship with Spencer. He had become quite the catch with his sandy blonde hair and rugged look. Although Claire swore that they were just friends, Ashley, Steph, and Jess knew better. They knew, without a doubt, that someday their friend Claire would snag one of the nicest—and let's face it—cutest guys in the entire middle school without any effort at all. Secretly, Claire knew it too, but she had no problem waiting until the time was right.

It turned out Ms. Jasper did divide the class into boy and girl groupings for the field trip, so Spencer and Claire weren't together.

Claire was happy to find that she had been placed in a group with Stephanie and Jessica. Ashley wasn't so happy to be separated from the others, but she managed.

Spencer wasn't so lucky. His friend Chad was placed in a different group, and the two boys in Spencer's group were in the band together. Spencer, unlike his best friend Claire, didn't have a musical bone in his body, so needless to say, he felt a little left out of the conversation. On the upside, they *were* interested in the special cat exhibit.

Spencer was fascinated by the different breeds of cats in the exhibit. There were coal black ones, fluffy white ones, leopard spotted ones, and striped ones. There were very small ones that looked like kittens but were full grown and others that were twice as big as Birdie. Some cats did not have tails and that surprised him. He gave the cats without hair a good long look and decided he liked furry cats better. Spencer had no idea there were so many different kinds of house cats! The exhibit brought back both happy and sad memories of Birdie. Through the months Birdie had been gone, Spencer thought of him often.

Claire enjoyed her time with her group. Their chaperone let her group take a quick spin through the small souvenir shop located just inside the front gate. As is often the case, the zoo gift store stocked items related to current exhibits. Clearly that went for travelling exhibits as well from the number of cat items scattered throughout the gift shop. Claire only had $7.49, so she focused her shopping on the small items in the bins near the front of the cash registers. When she saw it, she held her breath until she read the price tag that confirmed she could afford it.

"Oh, isn't that cute," said the clerk as she rang up the small keychain—a *gray* beanbag cat with a *black-tipped* tail. "Will that be all?"

"That's it," Claire said with a sparkle in her brown eyes. And without waiting for her receipt, she ran to the waiting school bus clutching the white gift shop bag.

* * *

Claire, wearing a satisfied smile, was one of the last students to get on the bus. She slid into the seat Spencer had saved her and said softly, "Gone, but not forgotten," and handed him the bag. Spencer pulled the four-inch beanbag cat keychain from the bag.

"I love it, Claire!" Spencer said, dangling the little cat from its silver chain. "Thanks!"

"I know your birthday and the anniversary of his disappearance aren't until February, but I knew I wouldn't be back here to get it. I thought you could hang it on your book bag. You know, to remember." Claire's words trailed off as both friends were lost in thought.

The day was extremely warm for late May. The bus ride was long and hot. Claire fought it for as long as she could, but almost an hour into the trip she gave in to sleep, her head resting on Spencer's shoulder. Trying not to disturb her, he leaned his own head on his crumpled jacket pressed to the bus window and gazed out at the tobacco fields with their broad yellow-green floppy leaves shimmering brightly under the hot Carolina sun.

CHAPTER FIVE

The White Ribbon

SPENCER WOKE TO A chime on his phone that signaled an incoming text. The message read

Meet me at the badminton net in 5 min.

He shot back a thumbs-up emoji and rolled out of bed, scrambling to find the jeans and tee shirt he'd peeled off the night before. He quickly brushed his teeth in the small bathroom that he shared with Rudy.

As he reached the bottom of the stairs, he paused at the mirror above the long, low table near the back door. His hair was sticking out in all directions, but he was one of those boys who could pull off the forever-messy look, so he simply ran his fingers through it and headed toward the door.

"Morning, Spencer," his mom called from the kitchen where she was busy mixing eggs into her batter. It was Saturday. Pancake day.

"Hey, Mom," Spencer replied, "Claire texted me. She asked me to meet her in the backyard. I shouldn't be too long."

"Well, invite her in for pancakes and bacon when you're finished talking," Mrs. Wilson said. "We've got plenty."

"Thanks, Mom," Spencer said as he headed out the back door.

Mrs. Wilson could see the backyard through her kitchen window. She watched Spencer approach Claire, who was already waiting in the yard. The Wilson and Champion families were good friends. Claire's older sister, Mary Jo, was a year younger than Abby, and her younger sister, Kate, was a year older than Rudy. Although Mary Jo and Abby weren't best friends like Claire and Spencer, they were good friends and spent time together around the neighborhood and at church. The same was true for Rudy and Kate.

But Claire and Spencer were inseparable and always had been. When their kids were small, Mrs. Wilson and Mrs. Champion used to joke about sharing grandkids someday if their two middle children ending up getting married.

Although Spencer and Claire were just friends,

both mothers realized that the possibility of the two kids ending up together somewhere down the line wasn't as far-fetched as it might seem. It wouldn't be the first lasting preschool romance in their small town, and it certainly wouldn't be the last. If something came of it, that would be fine with Mrs. Wilson. She thought the world of Claire and was grateful that her son had found such a true friend in her.

* * *

"Hey," Spencer said as he approached Claire. "What's up?"

Claire brushed away wisps of her thick brown hair that had escaped her ponytail and said, "Good morning, bed head. I have something for you." She handed him a small square box.

"What is it?" Spencer asked.

"Open it. You'll see," she said.

Spencer took the box and carefully lifted the lid. Inside the box on a bed of flat cotton was a narrow white ribbon coiled up like a tiny garden hose. The design on the ribbon resembled the crisscross pattern of a badminton birdie.

"What's this for?" Spencer asked, squinting in the early morning sun.

"It's a ribbon. For Birdie. I thought we could tie it in the top corner of the net to remember him. I know I just gave you the keychain, but that's to keep his memory with you when you're on the go.

This is to keep him watching over us here—like he always did."

"That's a great idea, Claire," Spencer said as he pulled the ribbon from the box, uncoiling it as he went. It was just long enough to make a simple bow when tied around the upper corner square of netting. Claire stepped back from the net after tightening the bow, and the two stood for a minute looking at it.

Two small girls, whose backyard connected to Spencer's, saw the older kids staring at the net and wandered into the yard to see what they were looking at. Spencer didn't know them well since their family had recently moved to the neighborhood. He did know that (although they weren't identical) they were twins and a little older than Rudy.

"Whatcha doin?" the red-headed one with freckles asked. Ironically, she was holding a raggedy stuffed cat that looked as if most of the stuffing had been loved clean out of it.

"Nothing," Claire said and then added, "What's your cat's name?"

"This is Pretty. Pretty Kitty. I've had her since I was a baby."

Spencer reached for the cat's paw and gave it a vigorous handshake. He said, "Well, pleased to meet you, Pretty. I can see you're a well-loved friend."

The twins giggled at the sight of the older boy talking to a stuffed cat.

"She is," said the redhead pointing to a bare spot in the cat's fur. "See, she's got another hole in her. Mom's gotta sew her up again!"

"Well, you let her keep patching up Pretty. Good friends are hard to come by," Spencer said.

And with that the girls ran back to their sandbox, Pretty Kitty dangling in the wind as they went. Although they were still kids themselves, Spencer and Claire felt big and grown and armed with wisdom from lessons that the two youngsters had yet to learn.

Looking at the ribbon again, Spencer said, "This is nice, Claire."

"I think we should do it every year when we set up the net for the season."

"Good idea," Spencer replied. And right there they vowed in the years following they always would.

CHAPTER SIX

Unless You're Dead or Dying

CLAIRE HAD BEEN PLANNING it for weeks. Her uncle had given her his old rowboat after he'd upgraded to a motor-powered bass boat. Since he had given Claire multiple lessons on boating safety, Spencer and Claire had gotten permission from their parents to take the boat out fishing at the large neighborhood pond. They also promised to wear their life vests at all times and stay within sight of their older sisters, who planned their own picnic on the shore.

Claire packed a picnic lunch of fried chicken, cornbread, apples, and chocolate frosted brownies. She filled a large thermos with sweet tea and sat on her back porch on her up-ended bait bucket and waited for Spencer.

Spencer was in his side yard hurrying to finish his chore of watering the vegetable garden before meeting up with Claire when Jeremy Boylan approached on his bicycle. Jeremy was a classmate who lived in the next neighborhood over. He had a reputation of being something of a bully.

"Hey, Wilson," yelled Jeremy as he readjusted his ballcap, "Me and some of the guys are going to Lake Side Park to play baseball. We need another player. You wanna come?"

"Nah, I can't," replied Spencer. "I've got plans to go fishin' with Claire." Jeremy turned his bike around and let his feet drag in the red clay dirt along the sidewalk to bring himself to a stop in front of Spencer.

"What *is* it with you and that girl?" Jeremy sneered. "What is she your *girl*friend? Do the two of you play Barbie dolls down by the creek or somethin'?"

"No, I...I," Spencer stammered.

"Forget it," Jeremy said and spun his tires spraying red dust as he tore down the road on his black bike with red scorpion decals.

Fine, thought Spencer. He ran inside and shoved a couple bottles of water, a cap, and his glove into his backpack.

"Spencer, is everything all right?" Mrs. Wilson asked when she saw him hastily zipping his bag.

"Everything's fine, Mom. Just fine. I'm going to Lake Side to play ball with Jeremy and the guys," said Spencer as he threw his backpack over his shoulder, grabbed his cell phone, and headed for the door.

"But I thought you and Claire..."

He couldn't hear the rest of his mom's sentence for the slamming of the screen door behind him. Once outside, he punched in Claire's name.

Claire had just about finished tying a new hook on her fishing line when she heard her phone ring from inside the house. "Claire, your phone's ringing. It's Spencer," Mrs. Champion yelled out through the open window.

"Not coming? Not coming, Spence? Why?" Claire repeated into her phone. "What do you mean something came up?" she asked. "Oh, I see," said Claire flatly. "Jeremy Boylan asks you to play baseball and you drop our plans just like that? You don't even *like* baseball, Spencer."

"But, Claire," he said. Nothing. All he heard was dead air.

* * *

"What happened to your date with your little *girl*friend?" Jeremy taunted when he saw Spencer walk on the field. Spencer saw a few of Jeremy's friends getting ready to play. Jeremy's little brother Kyle, who was the same age as Rudy, was there too.

Spencer felt sorry for the little guy having such a bully for an older brother.

"Knock it off, Jeremy," returned Spencer. "You need another player or not?" Spencer said, adjusting his pack higher on his shoulder.

"I don't know, guys," Jeremy said, looking to his circle of friends standing at center field. "You think we should let a *girl* play?"

Regretting that he'd broken his plans with Claire, Spencer said, "You know what? Forget it. I'm outta here."

"What's this?" Jeremy said with dripping sarcasm as he grabbed hold of the keychain hanging on Spencer's backpack.

"Is this your little *dolly*, Spencer?"

"Hey, let go of that."

Jeremy yanked the beanbag cat, and the chain snapped. "Why don't you go fetch your little kitty cat, if you ain't scared of the water, that is."

Horrified, Spencer watched as Jeremy Boylan wound up his best pitch and hurled the cat charm toward the small lake in the center of the park. But before the charm reached the water, Claire, who had followed Spencer from a distance, jumped from behind a large hickory tree, readied her best catch, and without even so much as a glove, snagged the cat right out of thin air.

* * *

When they reached Claire's house, Spencer finally broke the awkward silence. "Claire. I'm so sor..."

"Spencer Theodore Wilson," she said in a tone he'd never before heard her use, "unless you're dead, or dying, or want to be, don't ever break our plans again. Are we clear on that?"

"Yes ma'am," he returned in a voice so meek he was glad that Jeremy Boylan was nowhere around to hear it.

"Now," she said, her carefree voice back, "let's see about reattaching this keychain and loading up the boat. The fish are waiting."

CHAPTER SEVEN

Fun, Food, and Fellowship

THE CHURCHES IN BENTON normally did their own things except for once a year. Every Memorial Day weekend all seven of the town's churches would come together at the large community picnic area for the Koinonia (meaning fellowship) Festival in Lake Side Park.

Most people in Benton attended one of the seven churches, so it was more of a community event than anything. Even those who didn't attend church, like Jeremy Boylan's family for instance, were welcome and usually showed up sometime during the day.

Spencer and Claire, as members of the small

Baptist Church at the edge of town, had attended the Koinonia for as long as they could remember. Most of the other school-aged kids, as members of the larger Methodist Church just off the town square, had as well. Members of the other five churches were mostly older folks, except one congregation was made up of primarily young families with babies and toddlers. Regardless of which church you attended (or in the case of some, no church at all), at the Koinonia Festival everyone was family.

In May of Spencer and Claire's sixth grade year, the traditional event was planned as usual—carnival games, potluck supper, yard sale, pet parade (Max was selected to serve as the grand marshal along with Ms. Josephine Larson's chocolate Lab), bonfire, and fireworks. During the event planning, the committee asked each church to circulate a signup sheet for volunteers willing to do a stint in the dunk tank, auction themselves off for various tasks, or donate items for the tag sale aimed at raising money for the collective church-based benevolence fund.

Mrs. Wilson, being a lifelong Baptist, was always quick to volunteer her family members for anything and everything asked. By the time the Koinonia Festival rolled around, Abby was signed up to raffle off free babysitting, Spencer had an appointment with the dunk tank, Mr. Wilson was on the auction block for yard work, and every old toy Rudy hadn't nailed down was donated to the tag sale.

As it happened every year, Mrs. Wilson had deployed her troops in full force in the days leading up to the Koinonia. The evening before the event, she was in the kitchen baking cupcakes. Spencer's dad and Grandpa Theodore were in the garage nailing the final boards onto the grandstand backdrop, and Abby was in the den going through the bookshelves pulling books for the event's tag sale.

"Spencer," his mom yelled from the kitchen. "Can you go to the attic and get that box of old toys? It's high time those things made their way out of here."

"Yes ma'am."

"Thanks, honey. Do you need my help?"

"Nah, I got it," he said, stopping by his room to get his halogen flashlight.

From the quiet of the kitchen, Mrs. Wilson listened as her son ascended the attic stairs two at a time. Her thoughts drifted to old memories. Looking out the window above the sink, she scanned the creek bed on the other side of their wooded lot and thought about the many afternoons the family spent fishing and enjoying picnics near the rippling water.

She peered toward the back of the yard by the azalea bushes and crepe myrtles to see Spencer's badminton net. She smiled when she saw the white ribbon tied at the top and thought about Birdie. A soft sigh escaped from her as she noticed the old tire swing in the ancient oak. Grandpa Theodore had made it for his grandkids. Mrs. Wilson returned to her cupcake batter, smiling at the thought of her precious family.

"Mom," Spencer said, interrupting her thoughts. "Where do you want these?"

Mrs. Wilson reached for the box of old toys, "I'll take them. You should probably think about getting to bed soon. We've got a long day tomorrow. And I understand *someone* has an appointment with the dunk tank," she added with a wink.

* * *

The next morning, just before the sun came up, Spencer and his dad set to work loading boxes and baskets filled with Koinonia Festival items into the family's Ford Explorer. Mrs. Wilson emerged wearing black nylon running pants and a matching Nike tank. She was carrying a stainless steel thermos full of coffee and a brown paper bag packed with fresh bagels.

Claire and Grandpa Theodore were sitting on the front porch swing, rocking gently and watching the sun begin to rise. She was holding the small beanbag cat from Spencer's keychain.

"Hey, what are you doing with my cat?" Spencer asked.

"Looks like someone needs to take better care

of their belongings. It must have fallen off the chain again. I found it on the driveway this morning."

Spencer looked over his shoulder to examine the side zipper of his backpack. A silver chain with a couple of broken links dangled loosely. "Hmm, you're right. But you can't blame me. That's Boylan's fault for breaking the chain in the first place."

"No worries," Claire said, "I'll take it with me and reattach it to the chain when I get a break at the ticket booth."

"You don't need to do that. We can leave it here and do it later."

"Nonsense, it's your good luck charm. Might keep you from getting dunked!"

"Suit yourself," Spencer said, as he grabbed a box of cupcakes from his mom, who had just emerged from the house again, this time loaded down with boxes of baked goods.

"Whoever's going better hop in. We've got a lot to set up before the doors open," Mrs. Wilson said.

"Well, *he's* going," Claire said, waving the small beanbag cat in the air with a that-settles-it tone.

Mr. Wilson called out, "Okay, y'all. Let's hit the road."

Moments later the Wilsons and Claire were heading down the road toward Lake Side Park for the town's 35th Annual Koinonia Festival. Fun, food, and fellowship awaited.

CHAPTER EIGHT

Dunk or Be Dunked

THE FESTIVAL COMMITTEE MEMBERS were like a swarm of worker bees setting up for the event in the early morning hours before the opening bell. Boxes of tag sale donations were carted in and placed under the picnic pavilion as scores of volunteers unpacked the items, affixed price tags, and displayed them on the long tables that lined the pavilion in neat rows.

Claire threw a quarter on the tag sale cash register table for a small button basket marked twenty-five cents. She dropped the beanbag cat in the basket and set it on the end of the ticket booth table until she had time to reattach it to Spencer's backpack that was hanging on the back of her chair. Stephanie arrived and she and Claire began helping Mrs. Wilson set out the tickets, entrance wristbands, and the cash collection boxes.

"I think we're all set here," said Mrs. Wilson. "Stephanie, you hold down the fort, and Claire and I will go over to carnival games and see if they need any help. We've got just about thirty minutes before the opening."

"Okay," both girls said.

Claire and Mrs. Wilson made short work of getting the balloon dart game set up. As they took a second to admire their efforts, Claire saw a small line of festival goers had already formed in front of their ticket table, so she hurried over to take her seat beside Stephanie with Mrs. Wilson following right behind her.

Claire was amazed at how busy the ticket sales table was first thing after opening. It wasn't until about an hour into their shift that things calmed down enough for her to catch her breath. It was then that she noticed the basket holding Spencer's beanbag cat was gone.

Claire said, "Steph! Did you see a little cat thing in a basket when you were sitting here this morning?"

"Oh, yeah," Stephanie answered casually. "I assumed it was for the tag sale. I took it over there before you got back here."

"No!" Claire screamed, her heart sinking.

"Oh, Claire, I'm sorry—I thought it was just something somebody dropped off for the tag sale!"

"No, no. It wasn't," answered Claire in a panic. "I'll explain later. But right now, I gotta go get that cat back!"

Claire shot off like a bullet to the picnic pavilion and snaked through scores of bargain hunters in the direction of the toy tables. Her eyes darted from item to item, frantically scanning the mounds and mounds of playthings for sale.

"It's not here. It's not here," she said getting more desperate by the minute. Then she spotted a huge bin under the banquet tables filled to the brim with nothing but worn stuffed animals of all shapes and sizes. She dove at the bin, plowing through the critters with the speed of a cheetah on chase.

One by one, she threw the plush toys over her shoulder as she made her way to the bottom of the bin where most of the small stuffed animals and beanbag critters had settled. She knew she'd drawn a crowd of curious church ladies gawking at her with aghast expressions.

"It's not here!" she said for the third time. "Oh, silly thing! Where are you?" She knew how utterly ridiculous she must look to the audience that had gathered to watch the spectacle she made as she sat in a pile of castaway stuffed toys. She was on the verge of tears. Claire knew it was silly, but the Birdie charm had a way of improving the day if ever either of them was feeling down. Sort of chased away the bad.

"Dear? Are you all right?" asked an older lady, clutching a black vinyl purse.

"I'm fine," Claire sighed, getting up from the dusty ground. As she was putting the toys back into the bin, she caught a glimpse of a little girl at the makeshift checkout lane near the front of the pavilion holding a little round basket containing a small beanbag cat. Claire bolted to the cash table just as the little girl asked the Methodist lady running the show, "How much?"

"Ahhhh," Claire interjected abruptly, "that cat's not for sale."

"Excuse me?" the Methodist lady said. Claire knelt beside the young girl and said more calmly, "I mean, that cat belongs to a friend of mine. It got here by mistake. How about this? You and I can go back over to the toy table, and I'll buy you any other stuffed animal you want."

Claire, knowing she only had seven dollars in her pocket hoped that none of the toys were more than that, but she had no idea.

"Well," the little girl said, pointing to a large tie-dyed panda that looked like it had come straight out of a tacky midway game, "I wanted that one, but it's five dollars, and I only have one dollar. I was hoping this one would be less since it's so small."

"Oh," Claire said, with a quick glance at the girl's mother standing beside her for approval, "let's get you that panda then. And look here. I've got an extra dollar for you too. You can go get a snow cone!"

A minute later, the little girl gripped the panda with one hand and took Claire's hand with the other. "That's very nice of you," the girl's mother said. "I'll be serving at the baked goods booth. Would you mind bringing her to me after the snow cone?"

"Sure, I can do that," Claire said. The woman with the cash box stared at Claire with a *"that beats all"* look, but Claire didn't care. She had Spencer's beanbag cat back in her paws. That's all that mattered.

* * *

Before returning to the ticket table, Claire found Mr. Wilson over by the gospel music performers and asked for the keys to the Explorer. She took the beanbag cat back to the car and tucked him safely in the compartment between the two front seats that normally held loose coins and extra phone cords. "Enough adventure for one day for you," she said out loud as she slammed the car door shut and locked it behind her. *I'm taking no chances*, she thought. *He'll just have to be good luck from in the*re.

On the way back to the festival, Claire spotted the little girl from the tag sale. She was throwing her panda up in the air and catching it with sticky fingers stained purple from her grape snow cone. Claire chuckled and said, "I saved you from that, Cat. Looks like I'm *your* good luck charm."

Claire returned to the ticket table just a few minutes before her shift was to end. As she squeezed into her seat beside Stephanie, she was surprised to see Sheila McCalister in line to buy tickets.

Sheila was one of Jeremy's biggest followers and was every bit as mean as he was. Claire thought Sheila's jet-black hair, fingernails the color of coal, and that long, baggy, black trench coat she wore everywhere she went looked creepy. She shook her head at Sheila's painted lips, a purple so deep, it looked like blood. She was, in a word, a witch. She and Jeremy deserved each other as far as Claire was concerned. Claire forced a smile (it was the Koinonia Festival, after all) as Sheila and her band of rebel friends approached Stephanie.

"We need a book of twenty tickets," Sheila said flatly. Stephanie took the cash and handed her a string of bright green carnival tickets. "Thanks," she said as she snatched the tickets from Stephanie's hand with her black-polished razor claws.

Sheila snapped her head in Claire's direction, her snarled pitch hair swaying behind her like a matted horse tail. "We're taking these directly to the dunking booth," she shot at Claire, her words meant to sting like poison. "Your worthless friend's going down as soon as Jeremy gets at the baseball."

"All for a good cause," said Claire. Then she added with a slightly too sarcastic tone, "Enjoy the Koinonia."

She and Stephanie watched as Sheila and her tagalongs marched toward a waiting Jeremy near the dunk tank, the heels on their black boots sinking into the soft grass as they went. Just then two high schoolers from Benton Methodist bounded up. The taller one said, "We're here for our shift. Looks like you two are free to go."

Mrs. Wilson overhearing the exchange said, "I think Spencer's in the dunk tank for a few more minutes before the pet parade starts at the track. You might be able to catch the tail end of his shift if you hurry."

"Thanks, Mrs. Wilson! Let's go, Stephanie," Claire said and headed quickly across the field just in time to see Jeremy brandishing his roll of twenty tickets in the face of the dunk tank ticket taker.

* * *

"How many tickets for one ball?" Jeremy asked.

"Six tickets for one, or twenty for five," said an older lady from First Presbyterian.

"I'm sure I won't need more than one to make this shot, but I've got twenty tickets here, so give me five," Jeremy Boylan said with a smugness that was lost on the church lady.

"Get him, Jeremy," Sheila said as she watched

her leader wind up his best pitch.

Jeremy lobbed the ball at the small metal panel with a faded red bullseye painted on it. The ball missed the target by a mile, landing in the soft grass to the far left of the tank.

"Aw sh—" Jeremy began.

"Ah ah ah," the Presbyterian shooshed, cutting him off, "Watch your language, young man."

Jeremy cut her a look that was nothing remotely like Koinonia. This time, the look was *not* lost on her.

Spencer smiled wide from his small aluminum perch inside the dunk tank and said, "Is that all you got, Boylan?"

"The wind took it," Jeremy retorted with a quick glance at Sheila who had been videoing the dunk tank to catch the big splash.

Sheila paused the video recorder on her phone and said, "That's okay, try again." She hit the resume record button only to catch the baseball miss the mark again, this time landing in the grass to the far right of the tank. He knew better than to swear out loud this time, but anyone listening close enough, could hear the curse words voiced under his breath loud and clear.

Sheila hit the stop record button on her phone and shoved it down inside the large square pocket of her oversized black trench coat, which by the way, was just too much for the heat of the day.

Jeremy's next three balls missed the target

as wildly as his first two had. With each miss, Spencer just smiled, dry as a bone, on his small metal platform. After the final ball, Sheila turned to go, but as she passed the bullseye plate, she smacked it with her left hand, and kept walking. Spencer's perch gave way, and he plunged into the water below.

"Hey!" the Presbyterian lady yelled. "You can't do that!" But Sheila was already gone, her coattails flapping in the wind behind her.

A dejected Jeremy said, "Stupid dunk tank. That thing is rigged." He walked away with a huff in the opposite direction of his witch friend and her witchettes.

CHAPTER NINE

Yolk's on You

THE KOINONIA FESTIVAL CARRIED on through the afternoon in its usual fashion. Max outdid himself as grand marshal in the pet parade, the potluck was the best one yet, and the silent auction and bake sale raked in record totals. By the time the late day sun hung low in the sky, the crowd remaining at the festival gathered by the grandstand in the center of Lake Side Park for the culminating event before the closing fireworks show and bonfire.

The "Great Bandit Round-Up" was a favorite festival event for most. In fact, it was that event that caused everyone to stick around for the end of the day. The way it worked was simple. Tickets were sold for $1.00 each for a chance to serve as one of the five deputies allowed to "arrest" a bandit of their choice from the crowd. Five eggs were then randomly distributed among the winners, four hard-boiled and one raw.

On the signal, eggs were cracked on top of each bandit's head. The deputy that cracked the raw egg was declared the winner of the grand prize, and the egg-on-face bandit was given a cash consolation prize—encouragement for those selected from the crowd to agree to participate.

This year, Courtney Dickens' dad from Benton Feed and Supply donated a John Deere high-performance utility vehicle for the winning deputy, and the owner of the Stop 'N Go Mart donated a $50.00 cash prize for the bandit who "won" the raw egg treatment and a $20.00 gas card for each of the "losing" deputies. Needless to say, there was much enthusiasm over the chance to win a brand new bright green Gator!

Claire found herself right behind Sheila when she joined the line to buy her ticket for the event. Sheila gave her a sharp look and asked, "How many tickets are *you* buying?"

"Just one," Claire said, waving a crumpled one dollar bill in her hand.

"Good luck with *that*," Sheila shot back. "I'm buying a hundred," she said, flashing a Benjamin so crisp it looked as if it had come straight out of a birthday card from a grandmother. "Ain't no way I'm not getting picked as one of the contestants with a hundred chances. And when I do," she continued, "not only am I gonna take home that Gator, but you're going home with egg on your face. My hundred tickets will see to that."

"Maybe so, but it only takes one ticket to win," Claire said nonchalantly.

It took a while for the ticket taker to peel off Sheila's one hundred tickets. When it was Claire's turn, she handed the old man at the booth her dollar bill, and he peeled off one ticket—number 73219. She smiled as she looked at the last three numbers. *February 19. Spencer's birthday. That ought to be lucky,* she thought. She stuck the ticket in the back pocket of her faded blue jean cutoffs and made her way to the grandstand where Spencer was saving her a spot near the stage.

By the time the announcer walked to the microphone, the crowd around the stage had grown to six or seven people deep. Everyone was ready to hear the five lucky numbers called for not only a chance to win the Gator but also to have some fun with the "yolk's on you" event that had become a Koinonia Festival tradition.

With a loud squeal of the microphone and a crack from the old speaker, the event began. "Good evening, ladies and gentlemen!" the announcer boomed. "Most of you know me. I'm Pastor Matt from New Hope Fellowship. On behalf of the churches participating in this year's festival, we thank you all for supporting the Community

Churches Benevolence Fund by buying tickets to tonight's event. We truly appreciate your support! And now, without any further ado, let's get things started by calling the winning numbers."

Chad, the drummer from the Benton Baptist's praise band and one of Spencer's good friends, fired off a quick drum roll. Then Pastor Matt read, "7-3-3-9-8." The crowd responded with a collective groan except for one cheerful scream from the back. Peggy Watson from Oaks Chapel yelled, "That's me!" She made her way to the stage and stood behind empty chair number one. The next three numbers that Pastor Matt called danced around Claire's numbers, some close and some a mile away. Sheila, who was standing to the left of Claire and Spencer and three rows back could be heard as clear as a bell.

"Come on!" Sheila grumbled. "I have a hundred tickets here. One of those pulled should be mine!" Jeremy joined in complaining loud enough for all the crowd to hear too, until he was drowned out by Pastor Matt's booming voice.

"And now for the final number... can we have a drum roll, Chad? The final number is 7-3-2-1..." Pastor Matt was dragging out each number to a chorus of either "Aww!" (from those who didn't have the next number in the sequence), or "Yes!" (from those who did).

When Pastor Matt paused before the last number, Claire heard Sheila say, "Zero through eight...call any number but nine, and I got it!"

But, as if in total defiance to her desperate plea, the pastor hollered, "And the last number is...nine!"

Sheila said "What?! One number off!" Then she looked over to Claire who was smiling wide and waving the winning ticket wildly in the air. When Claire assumed her position behind chair number five, Pastor Matt asked the winners to declare who they wanted the "sheriff" to arrest.

When he came to Claire, she said, "Sheila McCalister, please."

Sheila shot Claire a look of pure malice, and then said to Jeremy beside her, "I better at least get the fifty bucks or someone's gonna pay."

As it turned out, Sheila did get the raw egg and the cash consolation prize, so her threat of making someone pay wasn't tested.

It was Claire who got the last laugh though. After she heard the satisfying crack, she pressed extra hard on the delicate shell grinding the slimy yolk deep into Sheila McCalister's jet-black hair. The tiny pieces of eggshell ran down Sheila's face in a river of clear white and yellow yolk. With perfect aim, Claire flicked the remaining shell bits from her hand toward the crowd below and watched with complete satisfaction as they landed smack dab in the middle of Jeremy Boylan's forehead.

She didn't stick around to see the seething look he shot her. She had already hopped down off the stage and up onto the seat of her brand new shiny green Gator. Another Koinonia in the books. Sweet, sweet fellowship with a touch of poetic justice.

CHAPTER TEN

Mittens and Boots

NOTHING IS BETTER FOR kids who live in the boondocks than to have a rugged all-terrain vehicle to cruise up and down dirt paths and alongside rows of tobacco or cotton. They learn early all about safety precautions when it comes to dirt bikes, four-wheelers, and ATVs. Since winning the Gator at the Koinonia, Claire and Spencer logged more miles on it than John Deere himself might have had he won the grand prize at the festival.

On one of their many adventures during the summer before their seventh grade, they rode down the path that led to the old Baptist Church building that had remained vacant since the parishioners had raised enough money to build a new facility closer to town. Often Claire and Spencer would stop by the old building and explore the abandoned structure and the grounds outside.

The old wooden pews were still in their original spots, and when the sun shone in through the thick stained glass, the whole room would light up in brilliant colors. All of the main doors were locked and bolted, but Claire and Spencer knew about the small cellar door in the back. It had a broken lock, so it was as good as the main sanctuary door if you were thin enough to make your way through the crawlspace and into the main building. Claire and Spencer both were.

On this particular adventure, when they slipped through the small cellar door and climbed up the basement stairs that led to the dusty wooden floor of the old sanctuary, they heard an eerie, hollow sound.

"What's that?" Claire said as the sound echoed through the old structure like the moan of a ghost.

"I don't know," Spencer whispered as he tiptoed toward the sound.

Claire, not to be left by herself, put her hand on Spencer's shoulder and followed close behind.

"I think it's coming from over there by the choir loft," said Spencer, pointing to the raised wooden pews at the front of the church. As the two cautiously approached, they caught a glimpse of what looked like a pile of soft, fluffy cotton. It wasn't until the cotton started to move that Claire and Spencer realized what it was.

Benton by any standard was a fairly small town. Population 950. But if you counted the feral cats, well, that was a different story. The stray cat community living out at the dam alone brought the town's population to well over 1,000 or better, if you were inclined to count cats, that is. What Claire and Spencer soon came to understand upon further examination of the moving cotton ball was that now two more could be added to the population count. The kittens looked to be about seven or eight weeks old. Their eyes seemed to have just opened.

"Oh, Spencer!" said Claire. "Look at how cute they are!"

There was no need to convince Spencer. Although Spencer loved his dog, Max, he was a cat person through and through. Both kittens were white, but one had two black front paws and the other had two black rear paws. They were extremely skinny. Spencer and Claire looked around the entire old building. No mother cat in sight. No signs of one either.

"Do you think they'd drink milk out of a saucer if we brought them some?" asked Claire.

"They might," said Spencer, "but I think I remember hearing something about not feeding regular milk or food to small kittens. For the weekend, we'll have to use human food, but we should probably stop by Gordon's Pets on Monday and get some advice." He bent down closer to get a better look at the kittens. Just as he did, the one with the rear black paws uncoiled itself from its comfy spot next to its sibling and padded over to Spencer's outstretched hand. An image of Birdie flashed in his mind. Spencer scooped up the little ball of fur and softly petted its tiny head with two fingers.

Claire quickly moved in to reach for the one with the front black paws. "Aww!" she said as she nuzzled the little kitten to her cheek. "Are you hungry?" she asked the tiny bundle in her hand. "I don't have any milk, but I know where I can get some," she said as she gently set the kitten back down under the old wooden pew where it had been sleeping.

"Let's go, Spence," Claire said. "We gotta get these fellas fed."

Claire and Spencer slipped back through the cellar door. They jumped on the Gator and zipped down the path that led back to town. Claire said, "I think we can get milk at my house to feed them. My sisters and parents are going to the mall. We can see if they've left yet."

As they came up alongside the creek that ran by Spencer's side yard, they spotted the Champion family car pulling out of the drive just as they cleared the tree line.

"Good," said Claire. "They're gone. We can sneak in and grab the milk without anybody asking questions. I can hear it now," she said, mimicking her mom's voice—"Don't you go feeding stray cats. Next thing you know, they'll be following you home."

Spencer laughed and said, "Well, my mom would probably cave and take them in, given how much she misses Birdie. But Max might have something to say about it. He's gotten pretty used to having the place to himself."

They both laughed at the thought of that. The Wilson's Golden was a giant baby. He'd gotten quite spoiled being the only pet in the house. As if on cue, hearing the four-wheeler approaching, Max bounded up to the pair to offer his friendly greeting.

While Spencer ran into his house to put Max away, Claire went to her house to grab a saucer and fill a travel mug with milk. Just as Claire was putting the carton of milk back in the refrigerator, Spencer knocked on the screen door and stepped in.

"I grabbed these," Spencer said as he held up a can of tuna and a hand-held can opener. "Maybe they'll eat a little. I grabbed this blanket for them too."

"Perfect," Claire said, "Did anyone at your house ask you what you needed with a can of tuna?"

"Nope. Mom was in the basement doing laundry, and everyone else was upstairs. Operation Mittens and Boots is still a top secret op."

"Mittens and Boots, huh?" Claire said with a smile. "I like it. I'm assuming that Boots is yours since Back Paws came to you first?"

"That's right," he said.

Claire grabbed the travel mug and followed Spencer out the back door to the waiting utility vehicle. Claire, anxious to get back to the kittens, kicked the Gator into high speed. In less than ten minutes, they were back inside the old church watching their new furry friends greedily lap up milk-soaked tuna like it was Thanksgiving dinner.

They stayed and visited with the kittens until late in the afternoon, watching them chase dancing colorful light beams reflected from the stained glass and bat soft dust bunnies that had gathered under the old oak pews. By the time Claire and Spencer headed back to town, it was almost time for dinner. They said their goodbyes and promised each other not to breath a word about OP-MB.

As Spencer entered through the garage door that led directly into the Wilson kitchen, he heard his mother saying, "Doug, did you eat the tuna I had in the pantry? I'm making tuna casserole for dinner, but I can't find it anywhere."

Spencer just put his head down and kept moving, but if anybody would have looked, they'd have seen a sly feline smile.

Poor Dad, he thought, *He's going down for this one, but I can't do a thing to save him without jeopardizing our secret.*

The family ate casserole that night, but instead of tuna mixed in with the peas, onion, and cream soup, it was made with some leftover shredded chicken that had been used in the chicken burritos a few nights earlier.

"This is good, Mom!" Abby said after digging in past the crushed potato chip topping. "You should make it like this all the time."

Rudy and Spencer nodded their heads in agreement. It was decided right then and there that the Wilson's would never have tuna in their tuna casserole again.

CHAPTER ELEVEN

Close Call

SPENCER AND CLAIRE ALWAYS sat together in church, along with Abby and Mary Jo in the pew right in front of the one that Rudy, Kate and the Champion and Wilson parents occupied. Just before the music started playing, Claire nudged Spencer gently in the arm and tapped on her phone to bring up her photos. The first one that popped up was of two furry balls of white cotton with adorable faces.

"I didn't know you took that," Spencer whispered.

"I snapped it just as you were leaning down to take a closer look at them," she whispered back. "I wonder what they're doing today."

"Duh," Spencer whispered, "they're in church,

like us!" Claire just shook her head at her best friend's witty humor, patted his forearm, and settled in for the long sermon.

And then, as if Preacher Samuel knew the deep, dark secret of OP-MB and the stolen tuna and milk, he said, "Good morning, dear friends. Today we will spend time in First Timothy, the second chapter, second verse. In it, Paul says, 'Pray that we might live a life of honesty.'"

Collectively, Spencer and Claire both gulped. By the time the last verse of the Doxology was sung, the two felt more than a little convicted, but they vowed to keep Operation Mittens and Boots a secret from their friends and family. And, along with keeping the secret, they knew that for the time being, they'd have to keep the mystery of the missing tuna under wraps too.

They rationalized it, however, by leaning on another verse their preacher loved to share, "For I was hungry and you gave me something to eat, I was thirsty and you gave me something to drink, I was a stranger and you invited me in." Armed with that, and downplaying their less-than-forthcoming stance regarding Mittens and Boots, Claire and Spencer—knowing they would have more nutritious kitten food soon—filled another travel mug with milk from the Champion's refrigerator and snagged a small can of pink salmon from the back of the Wilson's pantry (fingers crossed that it wasn't for a recipe on the schedule for that evening).

They headed out on the Gator to pay a visit to the stowaways living at the old Baptist Church.

* * *

"I'm not sure we can keep these guys a secret much longer," said Spencer one afternoon in August when they were on their way to visit the kittens. "With school starting, we're not going to be able to visit as often. Not sure how they'll get along without the daily attention. Not to mention, they're getting big enough to take off, I'm afraid."

Claire was just about to respond when she caught a glimpse of a large white van with green letters and an official looking seal parked out in front of the old vacant church. She grabbed Spencer's arm and pointed to it.

"Oh no," Spencer said as they got near enough to read the seal.

"Office of Animal Control," they said in unison. Two men came out of the old church, each carrying a dark gray cat carrier.

"Hey there!" Spencer said to the men, surprising Claire with his boldness. From the looks of them, they didn't seem like they were much for pleasant conversation. The taller of the men mumbled something that sounded nothing like a greeting as he followed his fellow cat catcher to the back of the van.

"Um," Spencer pushed, "You didn't happen to see two kittens around here, did you?"

"You trying to be funny, kid?" the shorter man fired back.

"No sir," Spencer said, his voice calm and even. "Seriously, my friend and I are looking for our kittens. We live just up the road, and they seemed to have wandered off."

Preacher Samuel's words about honesty came rushing back to Claire in an instant, but she couldn't help herself. "Yes," she interjected, "they go by Mittens and Boots. We've been looking everywhere for them."

"We're just doing what we're told. Somebody complained about some noisy strays. Boss told us to meet one of the church deacons here. He let us in. We gathered the cats. End of story," said the short one.

"But they're not strays," Claire said. "They're our pets."

"If these are really your pets, prove it. Describe them," said the tall one with a bet-you-can't tone in his voice.

"Oh, that's easy!" Claire piped up. "They're both white, but one has black on his front paws and the other has black on his rear paws."

The short man raised his cage to eye level and peered in through the silver metal grate. He turned to his partner and said, "I got two black rear paws here. What you got?"

The other looked into his cage and said, "Yeah. Two black front paws."

He said to Claire, "I'm guessing this is Mittens?"

"Oh, yes! Come here, Mittens!" she said reaching toward the cage, amazed at her own boldness.

"Don't your parents know that you need to get a tag on these cats?" the short man said. "Otherwise, they'll get mistaken for strays."

"Oh," said the two together, "we'll get on that right away."

Not until they were back on the Gator with their kittens tucked snugly in their laps did Spencer and Claire breathe a sigh of relief.

"That was close," Spencer said.

"Sure was," Claire responded. "Now, let's see if we can make it past the next challenge. You think our parents will let us keep them?"

"The kittens are pretty hard to resist," Spencer said as he gave Boots a little pat on the head.

To their delight, Spencer was right. That afternoon, both the Wilson and the Champion households grew by one. And as far as Max was concerned, you'd have thought he was part feline the way he took to the little kitten. The hungry, thirsty, and orphaned strangers had been invited in. Preacher Samuel would be proud.

CHAPTER TWELVE

The Munch Bunch

IN SEVENTH GRADE AT Benton Middle School one thing was unanimous among all the students—especially since the single-teacher set up meant you'd spend all your time with one teacher. You wanted Munch. You just did. Harris was a much easier grader, and she did some great units such as her fascinating Egyptian unit complete with a sarcophagus design project. But nothing could compare to getting in Munch's class. In fact, seventh graders at BMS actually renamed the schedule posting section of the middle school's website the "Who Got Munch?" page. Nothing else mattered. In seventh grade at Benton it was all about Munch and the luck of the random draw for getting into his class.

Munch and the Jackson County school superintendent, Dr. James Callahan, were longtime friends. Eight years ago, Dr. Callahan talked to his friend about trying out some of his collegiate research at Benton Middle School to see if it would make a difference in student performance.

Munch had, after all, spent the better part of his time while at the university as an education professor researching the impacts of giving middle grade and high school students what he called autonomy over their learning environment. He was a true believer in treating kids as adults so that they'd act like adults in return.

Dr. Munch and Dr. Callahan agreed to the arrangement, which was supported by the Board of Education, and so Munch continued his research through his new position as a middle school teacher, trying some unconventional teaching methods. The Munchers became his guinea pigs, for lack of a better word.

Since then, every year seventh grade students were desperate to find out if they'd gotten into the "community" come FDOC (pronounced f-dock), because immediately from the First Day of Classes, Dr. Munch set up his coveted classroom with a style that made the Harrisites green with envy. Just the fact that he called it FDOC, a term borrowed from college kids to label the start of a collegiate semester, told most of the story. Fact was, Munch treated each and every seventh grader fortunate enough to get the luck of that draw like, well, a college kid.

To say that Dr. Justin Munch was an eccentric character was an understatement. He wore thick dread locks tied back with a thin beaded cord and leather Birkenstock sandals even in the winter. He rarely wore traditional looking shirts, favoring loose-fitting smocks made from rough cloth. Whenever the kids at Benton commented on his eccentric look, he'd talk about what it was like growing up as the only black kid in his neighborhood in St. Louis and how it taught him to embrace thinking differently. That summed up Dr. Munch!

Munch was an expert at grant writing and reaching out to the larger business community to secure things for his students that no other classroom had. Educational grants Dr. Munch had received had paid for ultramodern furniture that looked like it had come from a free thinking, progressive tech company out of Silicon Valley. The clean white work pods had teal, blue, and orange rolling chairs that allowed the user to recline, swivel, or gently rock back and forth. Each workstation had personal charging ports, surround speakers, mood lighting, and other smart capabilities.

A state-of-the-art coffee bar that would rival any Starbucks in the country was in one corner of the classroom. It had flavored coffees, lattes, foamy café au laits, and earthy smoothies. Scones, thick slices of pumpkin bread, biscotti biscuits, and Morning Glory muffins were also available for purchase any given day. He had cleared the use of the coffee bar with the principal, after promising that he'd stock only decaf and limit a student's intake to one cup per day. As far as Munch was concerned, he left the responsibility for monitoring that to his students. No one asked. No one told.

So, walking into *his* room looked more like walking into a student union on a college campus than the florescent-lit sterile seventh grade classroom found in most of America's schools. With the ultramodern work zones and highly efficient coffee bar, Munch had his class set up like a well-oiled machine.

Students had rotating roles that they fulfilled each week in his class. Unlike usual class jobs such as recorder or timekeeper, Munch's student jobs served a real purpose. The barista had better learn how to make a caramel vanilla latte with extra foam just right or the "customers" would complain. The supply managers better not make a mistake ordering the milk, decaffeinated coffee beans, and pastries or Café Munch would close for business. The billing department better balance the accounts precisely or else the company that supplied the paper cups, lids, and cardboard sleeves would quit sending inventory. Yes, if Munchers didn't do their jobs, it meant real consequences.

Students in the Munch learning community

worked on group projects that were relevant, purposeful and, let's face it, fun. Munch didn't have tardy slips, bathroom passes, or late penalties. Students didn't get zeros for missing assignments, they didn't arrive late, and they never begged to go the restroom just to get out of class. They made what Munch called adult decisions, each one being responsible for his or her own actions. The fear of getting dismissed from the learning community (a consequence Dr. Munch had also cleared with the principal) was just too high to risk.

In mid-August before Spencer and Claire's seventh grade year began, they, like every other rising seventh grader, kept their eye on the "Who Got Munch?" page of the school website. Claire and Spencer were sitting in the loft area outside of Spencer's bedroom, checking the school site. When they pulled up the bookmarked page, they saw the red scrolling announcement bar marching along the bottom of the screen with the message, *Fall schedules now available. Login to the student portal to view.*

Claire turned to Spencer and said, "You go ahead. Pull yours up first."

Spencer's fingers danced across his laptop keyboard as he entered his password, *furballsRfun*. He waited impatiently for the tumbling hourglass to stop spinning. Seconds later, he was scouring his schedule for his homeroom class. Scrolling over to the right, his stomach sank as he read under the

Faculty column the word *Harris*. "Aw bummer," Spencer said with a frown. "I hope you get him though. Fingers crossed, Claire."

Claire glanced at Spencer with his goofy smile and crossed fingers waving in the air at her. It was moments like those that made her adore him even more. She never failed to lose sight of how truly lucky she was to have a friend like Spencer. He was thoughtful, kind, and always wanted the best for her, even if it meant they'd be separated in seventh grade.

When Claire logged into her account on the student portal page, she saw the name *Munch* in the highlighted field.

"Wow, Claire! I'm happy for you! Maybe you can sneak me a Munch Macchiato every once in a while," Spencer said with a genuine smile.

And she vowed right then that every time she could, starting with FDOC, she would.

CHAPTER THIRTEEN

Grazie, Signora Winters

THE MUNCH BUNCH GREW to be as tight as the Bunches from previous years in a matter of days. Claire was relieved to find that Jeremy, Sheila, and most of Sheila's witchy friends were not in the group. She felt bad for Spencer having to deal with them in his class, but at least their interaction would be limited. Kids in that class pretty much did their classwork independently.

In Dr. Munch's class, though, it was nearly impossible to avoid teamwork. With all the funding grants and waivers he'd gotten from the principal to try experimental teaching practices, the Munch Bunch was always travelling together, working on projects with one another, and engaging in team building exercises.

One such exercise was particularly thrilling. Months earlier, Dr. Munch set a meeting to discuss the idea with Superintendent Callahan and Mrs. Barrington, the school's principal. "I've found a really neat grant opportunity," he began. "There's this philanthropist from my hometown of St. Louis, Missouri. The family made it big in the popcorn industry."

"Oh, I read about that family," said Dr. Callahan. "They supply nearly all the nation's movie theaters with the raw materials for their popcorn."

"That's right," Dr. Munch continued. "The popcorn heiress matriarch—even though she didn't need to work—had been a schoolteacher for over thirty-five years. She said it was her sacred calling."

"So, they set up a foundation or something in her name?" asked Mrs. Barrington.

"Yep," Munch said. "After she died, her son established the Edith Winters Education Foundation. Their mission is to give grants to fund innovative educational projects that inspire students to become enthused, engaged, and lifelong learners."

"You think you can get one of these grants?" Dr. Callahan asked.

"I think there's a good chance," Dr. Munch said. He shared with his bosses his seven-page proposal that described in vivid detail his plan for taking his twenty-four students from Benton, North Carolina, to Florence, Italy, for a collaborative experience of geocaching with a group of thirteen-year-old Italian students.

"What's geocaching?" asked Dr. Callahan.

"It's the sport of finding the location of hidden treasure boxes using GPS coordinates," Dr. Munch explained. "People hide treasure boxes somewhere on public-owned land or in out-of-the-way locations in cities or towns. Then they enter the GPS coordinates on various geocaching sites on the web. Searchers then attempt to find the treasures following the GPS coordinates."

"Well, I for one hope you get the grant!" said Mrs. Barrington. "It seems like a great opportunity for our kids."

"For sure," Munch said. "The students will learn to work together using science, math, and technology as they search for their treasures in the *Italian* countryside!"

"You never cease to amaze me," said Dr. Callahan, extending his fist to his longtime friend. "Setting up a geocaching adventure is an innovative project in itself on *U.S.* soil. To couple it with international student pairs—that's another feat altogether!"

"We'll see," said Munch. "Fingers crossed."

* * *

When Dr. Munch received word a few weeks into the school year that his grant to take his students and five adult chaperones to Italy would be fully funded by the EWEF, he couldn't wait to tell the Munch Bunch. After a final okay from school leaders and clearing it with parents (sworn to secrecy until he told the students), Dr. Munch announced to his class, "We're going to Italy."

Most of the kids thought he meant virtually and so began gearing up for an electronic exchange with a classroom across the Atlantic.

"Nope," he corrected when Stephanie asked, "You mean virtually, right?"

"I mean we're getting passports (the price to expedite twenty-four passports would be covered by grant funds), boarding a plane, and heading off to Florence, Italy," said Dr. Munch with a mile-wide smile. Twenty-four ecstatic seventh graders, who could hardly believe their luck, bombarded him with a flood of questions.

* * *

Most of the kids at BMS knew about geocaching due to the large network of geocachers out by the dam. But Jess, who hadn't grown up in the area, didn't know much about it.

"What is geocaching?" Jess asked when Munch announced the plan, "It sounds fun."

"It is fun, but it's actually harder than it sounds," Munch said. "It's the sport of looking for 'hidden treasures' by using your cell phone to follow GPS coordinates entered on websites. A target hidden in a remote area or in deep woods can be a challenge to find, even after zoning in on the approximate location. Sometimes the target is gone—taken by previous groups or by people thinking it's litter."

"Oh," said Jess. "What do we do if we find it?"

Munch answered, "If you're lucky enough to find your target, you open the vessel to see what's inside! Sometimes there's a note or interesting items like a button, wheat penny, or seed packet left inside."

"What do you do with the stuff you find?" Jess asked.

"It depends," Munch said. "If there's a note, you fill in the date you found it. If there are objects in the box, you take one and replace it with one you brought."

"This is fascinating! And we're going to *Italy* to do this!" said Jess. "I can't wait!" The rest of the class chimed in enthusiastically. Most of them had not traveled much farther than their own state. An international trip was a dream come true!

* * *

As Spencer was riding along with the Champions to take Claire to the airport for the Italy trip he said, "Hey, you bought me a cat beanie keychain on our last field trip. Maybe you'll find a cool keychain for me in Italy!"

"I'll see what I can do," she said. But Claire was three steps ahead of him. She already planned to make finding him a keychain with some sort of Italian icon her first mission while in Florence.

* * *

From the moment Claire and her classmates landed in Italy, there were amazing things to see and do. They enjoyed lunches at quaint sidewalk cafes, visits to beautiful art museums, and walks through small Italian villages.

"This food is so fancy," Jess said as she, Claire, and Stephanie were sitting at a small table at an open-air pastry shop.

"What an amazing trip already, and we haven't even gotten to the best part yet—the geocaching! What did y'all bring for your treasure box? I brought this cat figurine holding an American flag," Claire said as she reached into her bag and pulled out the cat.

Jess said, "I brought a North Carolina quarter from the 50 States coin series."

"Cool!" Claire and Stephanie said at the same time.

Stephanie said, "Look at this!" as she showed her friends a bookmark that had a hologram image of the Cape Hatteras Lighthouse she had for her treasure box.

"No doubt, we have some good treasures to

leave behind. I just hope we find our boxes!" Jess said.

As the girls finished their pastries, Dr. Munch began circulating among the small tables to round up his students.

"You all need to be finishing up. We head out to meet our geocaching partners in five minutes. Here's the plan. We'll meet in a large park that has over thirty targets listed on the website. Teams will be assigned targets in close enough proximity to each other that the chaperones and I will be able to keep you in our sights during the search so nobody will get lost. The first team to find their treasure gets extra credit!"

Claire was thrilled to meet her Italian partner, Gabriella. After about an hour searching in the park, most teams had found their treasure. Gabriella and Claire were delighted to find theirs within about twenty-five minutes. Gabriella graciously gestured with a *you first* motion to let Claire select her item. Munch had told his students that their Italian partners would likely demonstrate acts of kindness as a way of showing respect to their guests.

Claire smiled and nodded a *thank you* as she looked at each item—a silver jingle bell, a thin paintbrush, a thimble, a small porcelain dish, and a faded card with a recipe written in Italian. *Definitely the recipe,* Claire thought as she smiled up at Gabriella who was nodding approvingly.

Claire tucked in her cat figurine with a note she'd written earlier. It said:

> I hope whoever finds this treasure box enjoys this cat figurine. I brought it with me from America.
> — Claire, Benton, North Carolina, U.S.A.

Gabriella carefully recorded the date in the small notebook and exchanged the small beaded bracelet she'd brought for the silver bell.

After all teams had returned to the rendezvous spot, the American students were treated to a tour of the school where their new Italian friends attended class. After the tour, the group walked together to a nearby restaurant for dinner. Munch used his best Italian, along with some of the Italian chaperones who spoke some English, to help translate when needed. But for the most part the new friends seemed to communicate just fine with smiles and gestures.

After a wonderful week, the Munch Bunch boarded the plane to return home to North Carolina. Claire found her row, stowed her carry-on in the overhead bin, and took her seat.

When the pilot announced that they had reached cruising altitude, she pressed her seat-back button to settle in for her long journey homeward. As she began to doze off, Claire wondered about the fate that awaited that cat figurine she left in the treasure box and thought, too, for a moment about Birdie.

She was glad that Spencer had Boots now, but she knew that Birdie would always hold a special place in Spencer's heart. She'd heard him say more than once, "Birdie had a way of chasing the bad out of a day." She thought about that a good long time. *I suppose a lot of us need the bad chased away from time to time.*

* * *

The trip to Italy proved to be all that Ms. Edith Winters would have wanted and more. The kids from Benton, North Carolina, experienced an unforgettable week while learning about friendship between people from two different cultures and how these friends could come together and learn things from one another that no textbook could teach. Each of the twenty-four Munchites brought back an entirely new appreciation of global awareness and a multi-cultural perspective.

When Claire stepped off the plane at Raleigh-Durham International, she was holding a small silver keychain in the shape of a boot. She knew the meaning wouldn't be lost on Spencer—the shape of Italy *and* a reference to his new cat, Boots. Not that he'd hang this one on his bookbag. One cat-related keychain was enough, but she knew he'd like it all the same.

The first thing she saw with her jet-lagged eyes when she made her way from the ticketed passengers' area was Spencer waiting with a red rose and a brightly colored mylar balloon that read *Welcome Home*. She smiled and ran to a welcoming group hug made up of Champion and Wilson parents and siblings.

Claire talked nonstop the entire way home trying to describe her trip of a lifetime. "I don't even know where to begin," she said. "The shops, restaurants, and houses were so different from ours. The streets were so narrow, and people rode bicycles everywhere!"

"What was the food like?" Mary Jo asked.

"Well," Claire said as she looked out the window as the car was approaching a string of fast-food franchises, "they had some of those places, but for some reason the food didn't taste the same."

"Well," said Mr. Champion, "what do you say we pull into that burger place for dinner and get you a good old American cheeseburger?"

"That sounds great," she said. To Claire, in that moment, there was no place like home.

CHAPTER FOURTEEN

Thirteen Red Ribbons

MRS. WILSON HAD BEEN tying red ribbons on the willow for a long time. Through the years, she had gone through a lot of ribbons of various shapes and sizes. She knew just when to buy her supply of ribbons. Immediately following Christmas and right after Valentine's Day she could usually find sales on seasonal stock. In preparation for Spencer's birthday, Mrs. Wilson headed to the store the day after Valentine's Day with a list that read:

milk
tomatoes
ground beef
elbow macaroni
devil's food cake mix

> vanilla ice cream
> laundry soap
> ribbon

As she headed to the back of the store, her eyes scanned overhead until she saw the *Valentine Clearance* sign. When she wheeled her cart down the aisle below the sign, she was pleasantly surprised. There was a huge supply of red ribbon spools. At 50% off, she couldn't pass it up. She decided to take them all! She counted the spools as she put them in her cart. Thirteen. *Huh, that's funny,* she thought. *Thirteen spools on Spencer's thirteenth birthday.*

And then she got an idea. Although she'd never done it before—tying the number of ribbons to match the age—she thought it might be fun. Thirteen ribbons for his first teenage birthday would make it extra special. She just hoped that it didn't give her husband the same idea on her birthday coming up in April. No way she wanted the neighbors counting that number of ribbons on Willodean. Woman and their ages, and all! But Spencer couldn't wait to become a teenager, so she knew he'd be thrilled to see thirteen ribbons on Willodean in just a matter of days.

* * *

"Aw thanks, Mom," he said when he looked

out the kitchen window that morning before sitting down to his bowl of corn flakes.

"One for every year!" she said, hardly believing that Spencer was turning thirteen already.

"Cake-cream tonight after dinner?" he asked.

"But of course," she laughed as she joined him at the table with her coffee and grapefruit half.

Spencer was looking forward to this birthday. Since it fell on a school day, he had opted for just a family dinner (including Claire, of course) with cake-cream that evening and then his party on Saturday. He smiled at that thought because it meant the thirteen red ribbons would stay up through the weekend, until he, his siblings, and some good friends went to the indoor rock climbing gym in Raleigh. Next to badminton, rock climbing was his best sport. He couldn't wait!

* * *

One thing about growing up in a small town is that everyone knows everybody, and furthermore, everyone knows what everybody drives.

"Well, would you look at that," Spencer said dryly as his family's Ford Explorer led the caravan of cars full of his party guests pulling into the parking lot of the Grip It Rock Park.

Claire, who had caught a ride in the Wilson vehicle, looked where Spencer was pointing and said, "What?"

"That red 4x4. Boylan's."

"Oh, no! Are you sure?" she asked, peering through the car window.

"Yep," he said. "See the Red Wagon bumper sticker from that famous county store over in Redmond?"

"Oh, yeah. You're right. They do have a Red Wagon sticker on their truck." Claire said, feeling terrible for Spencer. Of all days to run into the biggest bully from school. "Hopefully, we can avoid him," she said with a positive smile. "It's a big place."

Unfortunately for Spencer, the Grip It Rock Park wasn't big enough.

"Aw, how cute, Wilson," Jeremy Boylan said in a mocking baby voice as he saw Spencer's party entourage coming in the front door behind Mrs. Wilson, who was holding a half sheet cake and a bouquet of metallic balloons. "Will you all wear little party hats and blow on noisemakers?"

Spencer stopped in his tracks, inches from Jeremy, and said, "What did I ever do to you that you have to be so mean?" But before Jeremy could answer, Claire nudged Spencer along toward the party rooms beyond the check-in desk. Not really wanting a confrontation himself, he followed her nudge and moved along.

A positive, unintended consequence to Jeremy being there was that his little brother was also there. That meant that Rudy had someone to pal around with. Since he was being completely ignored by his older brother, Kyle was thrilled to see Rudy as well.

Kyle and Rudy had become best friends during the past school year. Kyle was a sweet kid—nothing like his older brother—so Spencer wasn't worried about his little brother's friendship with a Boylan.

In fact, Spencer hadn't shared with Rudy any of the ill feelings between him and his best friend's older brother. The smaller boys were so happy-go-lucky and innocent. Spencer didn't want to chip away at that, so he was content to let them remain oblivious.

All in all, the day turned out fine. The birthday guests were able to steer clear of the climbing walls that Jeremy was near, and Rudy had someone to hang out with in the section of the park for kids 4 feet 3 inches and under. When the climbing time was over, the guests returned to their party room for subs, plenty of chips, soft drinks, and birthday cake (this one store-bought). By the time they had finished eating, Spencer had nearly forgotten about his unfortunate encounter with Jeremy Boylan.

* * *

As the Explorer rounded the corner to the Wilson and Champion homes, Mrs. Wilson said, "Hey! Who ripped all the ribbons off the willow?

Who on *earth* would do that?"

Spencer was almost 100% positive he could answer that question, but he'd never been one to accuse. "I don't know," was all he said as Claire turned to him and mouthed the word "Boylan." A slight nod of affirmation in her direction was his only response. He'd seen Jeremy leave Grip It when the birthday guests were heading to the party room for sandwiches and cake.

According to Spencer's calculations, Jeremy had plenty of time to get home, ride his bike over to his house, rip down the ribbons, and ride off undetected. Classic Jeremy. Truth be told, Spencer felt sorry for him. *Something bad in there needs fixing,* Spencer thought. Problem was, he just wasn't sure what it would take to chase it away.

CHAPTER FIFTEEN

Love-All

THE ARRIVAL OF SPRING meant that it was time to set up the badminton net for the season. The two friends had decided that Claire would help Spencer set up the net first thing that morning. Around nine o'clock, Spencer texted,

Just got the net out of the garage. You ready?

Claire sent back a custom-made emoji face sporting a thumbs up. She grabbed the new white ribbon she'd bought earlier to tie on the net and headed down the stairs. With a farewell shout to her mom, Claire made her way out the front door.

As they replaced the old white ribbon in the top corner of the net with the fresh new one Claire had brought, Spencer was happy for the occasion to reminisce about funny things Birdie had done during their badminton games.

Once the ribbon was tied, they were both ready to get down to some serious badminton. Moments later, Boots wandered out the pet door and began to watch. He had been too little to come outside last fall before the net had been put away, so this was his first badminton experience.

Just like Birdie, his eyes were darting back and forth, following the lightweight cone as it made its way between the pair of rackets.

"Well, I'll be darned," Spencer said. "Maybe it's an innate Wilson cat trait."

Just then, they noticed that Mittens had made his way outside and had ventured across the quiet street to join the group. He stood on the other side of the net, opposite Boots.

"Love-all," Claire said as she set up her serve to begin their next game. Sure enough. Now not one cat but two intently watched for the birdie to drop.

"There goes your theory on *Wilson* cat traits," said Claire.

As they continued to volley, they watched the cats. Question was, when the birdie dropped, which would pounce first? Spencer decided to test the situation as he let the birdie drop. Turns out—just like Claire and him—when it came to badminton, the cats were hands down evenly matched.

CHAPTER SIXTEEN

Bluebirds of Happiness

THE REST OF CLAIRE'S seventh grade year proved to be as adventurous as the Italy trip, albeit on local soil. Literally. Local soil. In addition to Munch's thirst for providing purposeful educational experiences, he was also a huge environmentalist. He didn't just do a token Earth Day lesson on April 22 like many of the other teachers did. He made sure his students understood what it meant to live the experience.

Every Monday, weather permitting, rather than reporting to class, the Munch students met in the school's foyer wearing hiking boots and carrying walking sticks. They headed out through the woods on a trail that ended at the Hem River and the G.H. Glosser Dam. About twenty years earlier, the Army Corps of Engineers initiated a gigantic project to dam up the Hem for preservation, hydropower, and flood control.

Kids from Benton didn't remember the town pre-dam, but their parents and grandparents did. Some families told stories about their grandparents' houses that are under the 20 to 30 feet of water now known as Jackson Lake.

Water skiers, tubers, and jet skiers who came from Raleigh, Durham, and the surrounding small towns of Redmond, New Grove, and Curmont never gave it a thought as they powered their watercraft over what used to be whole neighborhoods and country roads snaking through Benton.

Munch had a whole unit on eminent domain complete with class visits to the homes of displaced old-timers who shared with the youngsters the impact the "damn dam" had on them back in the day. No apologies for the language either. These old folks told it like it was, to be sure. But, to the young families and those who scarcely remembered the history, Jackson Lake had become just a massive recreational and wildlife area to enjoy.

About a half mile from Benton Middle School, as the crow flies, sat the G.H. Glosser Dam and the Jackson Lake Ranger Station. Most kids in Benton casually knew the staff there, seeing them on occasion as they ducked into the ranger station to get a drink from the fountain or cruised through the small interpretive center displays of eagle eggs, beaver pelts, and stuffed raccoons. But the Munchers were on a first-name basis with the staff clad in drab green ranger attire.

Claire and Stephanie were particularly fond of Ranger Amy. Young and bubbly, she was a recent UNC grad who double majored in biology and environmental science and knew everything there was to know about animals, water, soil, and the great outdoors.

On this particular Monday in May, like all the good weather Mondays before, Claire's class headed to the dam for their outdoor education class session with their beloved Dr. Munch.

* * *

"Hey, Claire and Stephanie! How are you this beautiful morning?" Ranger Amy asked, handing them a clipboard with a list of the locations of all the bluebird houses on the property. "We're checking boxes today, girls!"

"Yes!" the two girls said in unison, pumping their fists in the air. Checking the bluebird boxes was by far their favorite task. It definitely surpassed trash duty. Seeing Ranger Hudson handing their friends Jessica and Ashley black plastic trash bags, they were doubly grateful for their luck!

Although the Northern Cardinal—known for the brilliant red color on the male bird—was the North Carolina state bird and was plentiful in and around the area, bluebirds were the focus for the rangers around the Jackson Lake Wildlife Area.

Claire and Stephanie enjoyed their time traipsing through the woods looking into each of the strategically placed bluebird boxes to check the status of the special songbirds that made the area their home. The girls diligently recorded whether each box contained adult birds, nests, eggs—or most exciting—baby birds!

The rangers kept a close eye on the statistics gathered by the student volunteers so that they could properly support the bluebird population in the area. To Claire, it was a beautiful thing to spend the day on the banks of the Jackson learning what it meant to be a responsible citizen caring for the fragile environment and the creatures in it.

Claire always said a prayer while she was walking through the woods, thanking God for all her blessings and the beauty around her. With the Carolina blue sky overhead and the Carolina bluebirds snuggled safe inside their wooden box homes, nothing could be finer. Nothing, except maybe for summer vacation. Which, according to Claire's calculation, was just a few weeks away.

CHAPTER SEVENTEEN

TK

SUMMER AFTER SEVENTH GRADE flew by. The only drama at the 36th Koinonia Festival was the record temperature that actually made a plunge in the dunk tank a welcome event. Spencer and Claire filled their days fishing, hiking, skateboarding, and—as always—playing badminton. Spencer was happy that Claire had such a great time in Dr. Munch's class, but as fall approached, he was glad they were finally moving on to eighth grade, especially when they found out they'd be back in the same class!

Rudy was even more thrilled with his class assignment because Mrs. Megan Wilson, his mom, would be his teacher! With the start of the new school year so near, the Wilsons made a special trip to the store to get school supplies. Abby was going into her junior year in high school, so she didn't need much other than some notebooks and loose-leaf paper. Spencer needed just a few more items than Abby. Rudy, as a rising Wilson second grader, needed lots of supplies like scissors, colored pencils, index cards, and a bottle of glue.

"Hey, Mom," Rudy asked, "will we really need all this stuff in second grade?"

"Yep!" she said. "We work hard. You better get ready!"

"Okay," he said, and then added a question that somehow failed to dawn on him earlier. "When you're my teacher, what do I call you? Mom or Mrs. Wilson like the other kids?"

"That's a problem every TK has," Spencer interjected. "Abby and I had it too, when we had Mom for second grade."

"What's a TK?" Rudy asked.

Spencer, surprised that Rudy hadn't heard them use the term before, said, "Teacher's Kid. There are ups and downs to it as you may have already figured out. On the upside, you get to go in the teachers' lounge and get soda pop out of the vending machine after hours while you're waiting for Mom to leave."

"Yeah, I did that some last year in first grade," Rudy said.

"Yep," Spencer said, "only TKs get to do that."

"What's the downside?" Rudy asked.

"You can't get away with *anything*!" Spencer said laughing.

"Well, I don't get in trouble like you, so I won't have that problem. It *will* be weird calling Mom Mrs. Wilson though," Rudy said. Then, turning to his mom he asked, "Ah, Mrs. Wilson, can I get this Batman lunchbox?"

She laughed at her son's wit, and said, "It's '*May* I get this lunchbox.' And sure, student, whichever one you want." They all laughed and carried on with their shopping, happy to be thinking about fall and more good times to come.

* * *

By the time the first day of school arrived, everybody was ready to start back. It took a little while for Rudy to get used to it, but he called his second grade teacher Mrs. Wilson at school and Mom at home. Rudy loved everything about his class. They made wonderful crafts, played games to review their math facts, and had friendly competitions spelling their vocabulary words. But the best thing about being in Mrs. Wilson's class was cake-cream celebrations.

Each month, the class got to help Mrs. Wilson make an ice cream log cake to celebrate the class birthdays in that month. Student volunteers were called to help stir the cake batter, slice the cooling cake baked in a cafeteria oven into thin layers, spread the softened ice cream, and best of all, roll the log! Being in Mrs. Wilson's class meant having a slice of the best cake on earth each and every month!

"Do any of your teachers at the middle school let you make cake in class?" Rudy asked Spencer that morning as he watched his mom loading the ingredients to make the cake for the September birthdays into her school bag.

"Nah," answered Spencer, "but we get to do other cool things."

"Like what?" Rudy asked with genuine curiosity.

"Well, dances, for one. Like the homecoming dance that's coming up. We get to go to that," Spencer responded.

"Dances," said Rudy, scrunching his face up like he just ate something sour. "Yuck. Who'd want to do that?"

"Just wait, buddy," said Spencer. "You will someday. You'll see." Spencer patted his little brother on the head, crunching the hair gel that held his stick-straight blonde hair in perfect place. Rudy reminded him of himself at that age. He remembered Abby having the *just wait* conversations with him too. He never believed her either when she told him he'd change his mind about certain things. Things change though. They always, always do.

CHAPTER EIGHTEEN

Badminton, Anyone?

ONE THING THAT HADN'T changed was the thorn in Spencer's side known as Jeremy Boylan. Spencer would have liked for the incident at Grip It to be his last encounter with Jeremy, but there were plenty of other unpleasant confrontations throughout seventh grade in Ms. Harris's class as well. And now that Sheila had officially become Jeremy's girlfriend, they were a doubly evil force.

Not that Jeremy and Sheila's announcement of being an official couple had any influence on Spencer, but he had been waiting for the right moment to ask Claire to be his girlfriend. Earlier that week, Spencer and Claire had planned a hike at the nearby state-run wilderness trail. What she didn't know is that he had snuck over to the trail before they began their hike and planted two small signs in the ground where the trail forked. One said *Friends,* the other said *Couple.* He was on pins and needles as they started down the trail together.

"Hey," Claire said as they came upon the signs. "What do you suppose those mean?"

"I'd say it means that a guy is trying to ask his *best* friend if she'll agree to be his *girl*friend," Spencer said with a you-got-me look in his eyes and his hand over his heart.

"Hmm," Claire said playfully. "Well, I suppose that guy will just have to see which path the girl chooses." She made a show of taking a few steps to the right, and then a few steps to the left.

Spencer held his breath until she crossed the threshold of the path labeled *Couple* and then took a few more solid steps down the trail. Spencer just stood there with a huge grin on his face as he watched her go. She turned around, her long brown hair glowing in the sunshine streaming through the trees and said, "Well, are you coming along, dingbat?" He ran down the path to meet her, grabbed her hand, and the two continued hand in hand on the happiest hike they'd had yet.

Now that Spencer and Claire were an official couple, he had hoped that he could keep his distance from Jeremy and spare Claire the drama. But, unfortunately, when you live in a small town, there is no getting away from creeps like Jeremy Boylan.

At BMS the physical education classes operated a little differently than at larger middle schools. Rather than separate boys and girls for gym class, the P.E. classes at Benton Middle were coed. The problem with that, according to the guys anyway, is that the sports were typically lame. Table tennis, floor hockey, volleyball, and sometimes even juggling.

"You've *got* to be kidding?" Jeremy Boylan said just under his breath the day the gym teacher, Mrs. Struggs, announced to the eighth grade class that they would be starting a fall badminton unit.

"Since this is a new sport for us," Mrs. Struggs began, "your grades will be based on sportsmanship and enthusiasm. I won't grade the practice games but will base your grade on the effort you show during the final tournament."

"Badminton? What the. . ." Jeremy sneered just *above* his breath this time.

"Mr. Boylan, do you have something to share with the class?" Mrs. Struggs's words shot like a bullet.

"No ma'am," Jeremy replied with a sideways glance at his classmates that said, *You laugh, you'll be sorry.*

"Very well," replied Mrs. Struggs, and then the class spent the next forty-three minutes hearing about how the badminton unit would last several weeks and culminate in a grade-wide tournament crowning the top male/female team the badminton champs of Benton Middle School. If Jeremy's eyes would have rolled farther back in his head, he'd have been dead.

"Spencer!" Claire said at lunch after gym class, "This is awesome. You and I both know we're going rock this badminton thing."

They were good. It had been years since Spencer's parents had been able to beat them. Abby and Mary Jo wouldn't even play against them. "This is our chance to smash Jeremy Boylan, literally! Everybody knows that if there's a trophy involved Boylan thinks it's his," Claire said. "It doesn't matter to him if it's a cardboard golden racket like this time or a silver prize cup. He thinks he's entitled. But not this time. This trophy is *ours*!"

"No so fast, Claire," Spencer said with a look of mischief. "I think we should...how should I put this...? Take the practice games less than seriously."

"What are you saying, Spencer? You want us to *lose* the warm-up games?" Claire asked looking at Spencer like he'd lost his mind.

"Not just lose, Claire. Lose bad. Humiliatingly bad," he said with a sly smile.

"Do I even *want* to know?" said Claire, shaking her head resignedly.

* * *

Mrs. Struggs let the students select their own partners so, naturally, Spencer picked his now official girlfriend, Claire. Jeremy picked his wicked girlfriend, Sheila.

The day the practice games started, Claire followed Spencer's plan to the letter. She made a dramatic show of running wildly after the birdie she never seemed to catch. Spencer would purposely miss his serves and then look down at his racket as if it had a hole in it. They ducked, screamed, fell down, dropped their rackets, even bumped smack dab into each other in the practice sessions, all without ever hitting the little white birdie where it needed to go.

Each day after gym class they laughed themselves silly. Their close friends knew they were much better players than they were letting on, but they assumed there was a ruse going on and never let the cat out of the bag. Spencer and Claire agreed they'd just have to convince Mrs. Struggs that they put in plenty of out-of-class practice time so she'd attribute their huge improvement at the tournament to just that. They were sure they could.

"Hey, Jeremy," Spencer said the day before the tournament was to begin, "I was thinking about a little wager. On the badminton tournament. You interested?"

"We're not allowed to bet at school," Jeremy said dryly.

"Oh, it doesn't have to be for money," Spencer said. "I was thinking more for a privilege."

Jeremy was the current student government representative at BMS for their grade level. As their rep, he was tasked with recommending to the faculty advisor the eighth grade homecoming king and queen, who got to ride in the horse-drawn carriage in the homecoming parade. Everyone knew that rarely did the advisor challenge the student recommendation, so for the most part, whatever the rep suggested was usually the final word.

The town of Benton hadn't always had an eighth grade king and queen in the homecoming parade. It used to be just the high school couple elected from the senior class. Claude Hanson, the owner of the local car dealership, Hanson's Chevrolet, always offered a shiny new convertible—with a giant Hanson's Chevrolet placard plastered on the side—for the senior couple to ride in. But a few years back, an eighth grader named Courtney Dickens, a born drama queen, was pouting to her daddy about how unfair it was to have to wait until high school to be named homecoming queen.

Since Courtney's dad owned the local feed store (Mr. Dickens was the one who donated the Gator for the Great Bandit Round-Up at the 35th Koinonia) and was on the school board, it was quickly decided that the eighth graders would name a royal pair to be represented in the parade. Benton Feed and Supply arranged a horse and carriage for the junior couple to ride in, and naturally, Courtney and her boyfriend, Bo, were crowned the inaugural couple. After that, the eighth graders had a king and queen of their own, and they always rode in a horse-drawn carriage in the town parade. Politics in a small town. No way around it.

Everyone at Benton Middle knew that Jeremy would nominate himself and Witch Woman Sheila to be this year's junior king and queen. Everyone also knew that the faculty advisor wouldn't bother to challenge his nomination, so it was as good as done. That's why it was easy bait when Spencer proposed casually, "A wager, you know, on the tournament. Between us four, you nominate the winners as homecoming couple. The couple that wins will be named king and queen and the couple that loses will walk behind the carriage with a shovel and pick up, you know, the horse's... droppings."

"You and Claire are going shovel horse crap behind our carriage?" said Jeremy with a belly laugh.

"If we lose," said Spencer evenly.

"*When* you lose, Wilson. When you lose. You're on," he said smugly. And then Jeremy Boylan made a colossal mistake. He turned to his classmates and said, "Can we get a witness to this? I don't want Wilson weaseling out of this bet when he and his freak girlfriend go down."

A half-dozen kids responded, "We got it, Jeremy. This deal's goin' down."

* * *

Claire looked more beautiful in the emerald green satin dress she'd selected for her royal ride as eighth grade homecoming queen in the town parade than Spencer ever imagined. She was equally blown away by the way he looked in his new charcoal gray suit. Just before the carriage was ready to pull out onto the parade route, Spencer handed Claire a small box.

"What's this?" Claire asked as she opened the lid.

"It's just a little present," Spencer said. "You're always getting me things. It's your turn to get something!" Inside the box was a gold barrette with small pearls.

"Oh, I love it, Spencer!" Claire said as she replaced the plain clip that was holding her hair back with the beautiful new clip. She turned so Spencer could see. "How's it look?" she asked.

"Perfect, Queen Claire," he said. With pearls in place and dressed to the hilt, the couple would have looked utterly graceful except for their bursts of hysterical laughter each time they looked behind their carriage and saw Jeremy Boylan, wearing his father's pond waders, scooping massive mounds of steaming horse poop into the metal pail dangling from Sheila McCalister's jet black fingernails.

After all, a bet is a bet.

CHAPTER NINETEEN

Rudy

TO CELEBRATE THEIR VICTORY, and because they knew there wouldn't be many more days in the late fall before it got too cold to fish, Claire and Spencer set out once again for their favorite pastime with poles and buckets to their fishing spot at the creek bordering the north side of Spencer's backyard.

Rudy saw them getting ready and begged to go along. He idolized his big brother, and he adored Claire too. But a noisy, energetic seven-year-old is the last thing the two had in mind for the lazy, quiet afternoon. Not to mention that Rudy's habit of traipsing through the water to catch bullfrogs would most definitely scare the fish away.

"Not this time, bud," Spencer said gently.

"Yeah, kiddo," Claire added. "We'll plan a day of frog catching soon!"

Rudy, satisfied with the promise of a future outing, bounded off in the direction of the tire swing that Grandpa Theodore had made when Spencer was small.

Claire and Spencer fished for a long while without so much as a tug on their lines, but they were content to stay regardless. Claire, spying Rudy playing on the tire swing, said, "I feel bad that we didn't bring him. He's such a cutie pie. I can't believe he'll be eight soon."

"Yeah," said Spencer exhaling a deep breath. "Another birthday. Another ribbon on Willodean. And it will be *two* cake-creams for Rudy this year. One in class for the monthly birthday celebration and another one at home."

"That's right. I remember getting those cake-creams in second grade."

"Yep. All the Wilson kids came to know that the year that teacher was also Mom, you hit the birthday jackpot in terms of cake-cream!"

"I'm sure Rudy is excited about that," Claire said. "Have you decided what to get him?"

Spencer had been thinking about what to get Rudy for some time. Spencer knew how much Rudy looked up to him as an older brother, so the perfect present from him was important.

"Not sure," he said. "I've been racking my brain. Rudy likes his bike. Rudy likes to fish. Rudy loves joining us on hikes in the woods."

On those outings in the woods on the public lands surrounding the dam, Rudy would typically spend the first half of the hike looking in the brush for the perfect hiking stick. He was always saying that he was going to take his stick home and get his dad to help him sand it down and varnish it so that it looked like the shiny professional hiking sticks he'd seen in the outfitter shops in Boone or Asheville.

But he'd invariably set his stick down while catching bullfrogs or when they'd stop at a picnic shelter for a snack and then leave it behind when they continued on the hike. Spencer joked that Rudy's stick needed a pair of Army dog tags so the next hiking battalion that happened upon it would know where to return the missing "soldier." It had become their standing joke.

"That's it, Claire!" said Spencer. "The perfect present."

"What is?" she asked, not sure exactly what Spencer was thinking.

"A hiking stick! A Rudy-sized, natural, woodsy-looking hiking stick that he won't lose in the woods! And I'll see if I can find some Army dog tags to wrap around the stick!"

When it was clear that the fish weren't biting, the two packed up their gear and headed back up to Spencer's house. Sitting on the balcony outside his room, they turned to the internet to search for kid-sized hiking sticks.

"This one is perfect," Spencer said to Claire who was sitting cross-legged on the floor next to him.

"Yeah," Claire said. "Put it in your cart, and now let's look for dog tags," she whispered as Rudy was in his room just a few feet away.

Spencer continued his search by typing *decorative dog tags* into the search bar. "Here we go," he said as he pointed the screen in Claire's direction. There was a whole page of options for Army-like dog tag "necklaces" that would be perfect to wind around the top of a small walking stick.

"Oh, yes! This is great," Claire whispered. "It says here that you can get *custom* tags shipped in two days."

Spencer was just about to ask his mom for her debit card to purchase the tags and stick online when he and Claire overhead Rudy and Mom in Rudy's room. Rudy was crying. Through his tears he said, "I don't understand why he won't come. He's my best friend."

"Well, what did he say? Did he tell you why he can't come? Maybe he has a good reason."

"No, he doesn't," Rudy cried. "He said his big brother said that I was stupid, and that everybody will think he's stupid too if he comes to my party."

"Honey, that doesn't seem like something his older brother would say. Are you sure that's what he said?"

"Yep," said Rudy sadly, "and no matter how

many times I ask him to come, he still says no."

Spencer's heart sank. He looked at Claire and said, "Boylan."

She nodded in understanding. He ached for his little brother and wished there was something he could do. But there was no wager on a badminton tournament or raw eggs at a festival to get the better of Jeremy Boylan this time. This time it seemed the bully had won.

CHAPTER TWENTY

Help

MOST SMALL TOWNS HAVE an urban legend about some mystery that happened out at the water tower or town reservoir. Or there is that old vacant house or barn behind a tall fence or at the end of an old road that kids dare each other to venture down, only to find nothing particularly spooky about it when they get there.

Benton had one of those legends. For years, kids talked about the old Stevenson Place out beyond the water tower *and* the reservoir that was said to be haunted. Through the years, daring kids would venture out there to explore the ten or so acres that surrounded the place.

Some trails on the property were fairly well established and easy to navigate. Others were less obvious and were hugely overgrown. The property was fully surrounded with a heavy wrought iron fence, so it wasn't possible to get completely lost. Eventually, given enough time, you'd come to the front gate if you knew to follow the fencing around the acreage.

Claire and Spencer had gone out there a couple of times, but it didn't hold much appeal to them. They preferred to hang out and fish at the reservoir located just south of the property. In fact, that's exactly where they decided to spend their day. Earlier that morning, Spencer met Claire at her house with his pole and tackle box. She already had her stuff loaded and was on the Gator when he arrived.

"Think it's gotten too cold for the fish to bite?" she asked as he slid onto the front seat next to her.

"Nah, it's been pretty warm lately. Something ought to bite. And speaking of the fish biting, I brought you something!"

Claire took the small paper bag that Spencer held out to her. "Aw, Spence! What a cool lure. Thanks!"

"I thought you'd like the florescent green color."

Claire laughed and said, "I love it!"

They headed down the dirt path that led out toward Old Stevenson Road. When they arrived, they parked the Gator at the entrance to the reservoir. Not many people came past the area unless it was the county utility workers checking on the water levels or kids on their way to find mischief at the old Stevenson Place. Either way, the Gator would be safe so long as Claire took the key. Nobody could run off with it if they couldn't start it.

The couple had been fishing for about an hour and had been having quite a bit of luck with the small mouth bass and crappie. "I could stay here all day," Spencer said after landing his third bass.

"Me too," Claire said as she took a careful drink of hot cocoa from her stainless steel Yeti.

Spencer jumped a bit when his cell phone rang. "I'm not even gonna get that. It's probably Chad wanting to do something," he said. "I know better than to even *think* about getting lured away from fishing with you after that time with Boylan," he said playfully.

When the phone stopped ringing, Spencer said, "See, it wasn't important."

Claire smiled and offered him her thermos of hot chocolate. He was just about to take a sip when his phone started ringing again. This time he glanced at it. "It's not Chad," he said with mild curiosity. "I don't recognize the caller, but it is a Benton number."

"Well, answer it then. See who it is," Claire said.

"Hello?" Spencer said into the phone.

"Wilson," came the response on the other end of the phone, "It's me—Jeremy. Listen. I need your help. Sheila and I came up to the old Stevenson Place this morning, and we saw Claire's Gator as we passed the reservoir. Are y'all still out there?"

"Yeah..." Spencer said tentatively. "What's wrong?"

By this time Claire was whispering, "Who is it? Who is it?"

Spencer covered his phone with his hand and mouthed, "Jeremy Boylan." Then he put it on speaker so that Claire could hear.

Jeremy said, "I know I'm the last person that you'd expect to ask you for something, but I really need your help. It's Kyle. My little brother."

At that, Claire and Spencer could hear real panic in Jeremy's voice and knew he wasn't playing games.

"I was supposed to be watching him for my mom, but Sheila and I had plans to come up here to the vacant house, so we brought him with us. I told him to stay by the front gate and play his video game while we hiked the back trail. When we got back, he was gone.

"We've been searching for about ten minutes, calling for him. Nothing. I'm really scared. The creek out here is running high. We'd cover more ground and quicker if you brought the Gator up here."

"Boylan," Spencer said, "call your parents! Your dad has a Polaris. That'll do even better on the trails out there anyway. Heck, you should probably call the Volunteer Fire Department. They'll come out and help."

"No. I know I should," said Jeremy, "and I promise I will if we can't find him after fifteen minutes searching the trails using Claire's Gator. It's just that I'm in so much trouble with my parents already. I got suspended from school last week for skipping detention, and I got caught sneaking out of the house last night after curfew. I'm actually grounded right now. They'll kill me if they know I left the house...and took Kyle. Please, Wilson, I'm begging you."

Spencer had never heard Jeremy Boylan sound so vulnerable since he'd known him, and that was practically his whole life. He looked at Claire who was slowly nodding her head in a *yes-we-do-this* way.

"Okay," Spencer said. "We'll be right there."

"Thanks, Wilson. Thanks," came the response from Spencer's worst enemy in the entire world.

The four searched the old Stevenson Place property for about ten minutes, calling Kyle's name repeatedly. At one point, Spencer looked over his shoulder to the back seat of the Gator to see that Sheila was crying. He stared in awe when he saw Claire take her hand and whisper, "We'll find him."

Minutes seemed like hours as the Gator inched along the worn path. Just then, a tiny voice rang out from an area with thick underbrush.

"Jeremy! Sheila!" came Kyle's voice.

"Stop, stop!" Jeremy yelled. "I hear him!"

Spencer had heard him too and was already stopping the ATV. Jeremy jumped down and ran toward the voice. What Spencer saw next was a tenderness and caring that he never thought he'd see from Jeremy Boylan in all of his life.

"Squirt," Jeremy said hugging his brother like he was long-lost Lassie. "Why'd you leave the gate?"

"I got scared. I went looking for you."

"I'm so sorry we left you, champ. We're so glad you're all right," Jeremy said, exhaling in relief.

"Hop on, little man," interjected Spencer. "Let's get y'all home."

"Nah," said Jeremy, "we got our bikes."

"No problem," Claire said, "we'll take you home, and then Spencer and I will come back here and get them with the Gator. We'll drop them alongside of your garage. Nobody will ever know you were gone."

"Thanks, you two," Sheila said as she turned to give Claire a hug as if they'd been doing it their whole lives.

When the five arrived back at the Boylan house, Sheila said, "Claire, can you help me get him in and settled?"

"Sure," Claire responded. She grabbed Kyle's backpack and his handheld video game and followed Sheila through the garage door into the house. Jeremy awkwardly offered his hand to Spencer. Spencer took it and shook it vigorously.

"Thanks, man," Jeremy said, bowing his head low. "Thanks. I don't know what else to say. I mean, I owe you. Anything. You name it. I owe you."

"There *is* something you can do for me," Spencer said.

"Anything. You name it. It's yours," returned a still trembling Jeremy.

"Just convince Kyle to come to Rudy's birthday party next week. Tell him *you* were the stupid one," said Spencer with a slight smile.

Jeremy hung his head even lower. "Yeah. I hate that I did that. Yes, of course. He'll be there."

"Hey," Spencer added, "you and Sheila come too. We'll hang out in the bonus room. I got the newest version of RuSH III. We'll play it as teams. See if you can beat us."

"You care to place a wager on that?" Jeremy asked with the most genuine smile Spencer had ever seen cross his former enemy's face.

"You're on," replied Spencer. A stranger thing had never happened to Spencer Wilson in all of his days.

CHAPTER TWENTY-ONE

Willodean Adorned Again

A WEEK LATER, RUDY popped out of bed just as the sun was breaking on the horizon. He ran to his window and tugged at the blind strings.

There it was. The ribbon. It didn't matter how early the birthday boy or girl jumped out of bed to peer out the window, the ribbon was always there. It was as dependable as the tooth fairy's dollar under the pillow or Santa's filled stockings.

Nobody ever gave it a second thought, except Mrs. Wilson that is. She had snapped awake at three a.m. a time or two with the realization that she'd forgotten to sneak a ribbon on the willow for the morning reveal. It didn't matter if it was freezing cold, pitch dark, pouring rain, or blazing hot. She never failed to get the job done on time. She was a stickler. She said that's what made a family tradition a tradition.

So yes, the ribbon was there when Rudy awoke.

For this occasion, however, Mrs. Wilson broke with her tradition of keeping birthday parties simple and caved on Rudy's request for a big party. And a big party it would be. Loads of family and tons of friends would be there.

And most importantly, Kyle would be there. Jeremy and Sheila too. But anyone who had seen the couple a mere week earlier wouldn't have recognized them on this day. The incident at the old Stevenson Place had changed them in so many ways. For Jeremy, the change was mostly evident in his manner. The kid who previously wore the abrasive, tough bully exterior had virtually disappeared, replaced by a quieter guy with a genuine smile.

Sheila changed both inside and out. In fact, when she arrived at the party, Spencer didn't even recognize her.

"Can I help you?" he said after answering the door. Since he knew all the kids on the guest list, he assumed she must be lost or looking for a different house in the neighborhood.

"Hey, Wilson," she said. Spencer racked his brain. The attractive girl in front of him was vaguely familiar. The voice. He knew that voice, but he just couldn't quite place her.

"It's me. Sheila. Sheila McCalister?" she said with a question in her voice that hinted *you don't recognize me, do you?* He peered at her through squinted eyes, his mind trying to add back the stark black hair, coal black fingertips, and blood purple lips. He almost couldn't do it. The girl standing at the door had soft blonde hair, was wearing a pure white fleece jacket, and had pale pink polish on her nails.

"I know, I know," Sheila said, nodding her head as she spoke so that the soft blonde curls bounced gently across her shoulders. "I decided to change my style. Dyed my hair. Lost the creepy look. Jeremy likes this better. Imagine that."

"Oh," was all he could manage to say as he was still trying to compute that the girl before him could actually be Sheila McCalister.

"He'll be here in a little bit with Kyle..." she trailed off. She added hesitantly, "So, are you going to invite me in?"

"Oh, yeah, sorry," Spencer said as he held the door open wider to allow Sheila to step past him. "You're right," he continued, "I didn't recognize you. It's a good look."

"Why thank you kindly," Sheila said with a mock Southern curtsy that, for the life of him, Spencer could never have imagined coming from Sheila-the-Witch McCalister.

Just then, there was another knock on the door.

Jeremy. Spencer was glad he hadn't dyed his hair and done a complete 360 with his wardrobe. But all the same, it was almost equally hard to recognize the new Jeremy.

"Welcome," Spencer said holding the door open. "Kyle," he added, "Rudy's been waiting for you! He's in the living room."

The younger kids gathered in the den, while the older kids gravitated to the kitchen. Eventually the party got underway with everyone filling their plates with mounds of pepperoni pizza and potato chips. Mrs. Wilson had made an extra-long cake-cream so there would be enough for all the party guests. After Rudy blew out his candles atop the log, he blurted out, "I wish for more cake!" That set off a ripple of laughter as everyone eyed the huge cake-cream that Mrs. Wilson had made.

After all the guests had finished their pinwheel slices of cake-cream, Rudy tore into his small mountain of presents. Sheila, Jeremy, Claire, and Spencer were seated in the far corner of the room, lost in their own conversation. They had been talking nonstop since the party began. A casual observer who didn't know their history would have thought they'd been friends forever, but the truth was it was about as unlikely a grouping as a Duke fan, a Carolina fan, and a State fan together at pregame tailgate.

They relived some of the mean and dirty tricks they'd dished out to each other over the years. They reminisced about the pranks that had been played *by* various kids *on* various kids throughout their elementary and middle school days. But what plunged them into hysterics more than all the rest is when they thought back to the badminton tournament. It had just been about a month ago, but with all that had happened, it seemed like years.

The new Jeremy, while laughing at himself along with the others, had to admit to Spencer that it *was* a good one.

"Just wait until you see what Kyle brought Rudy for a present. I helped him pick it out." said Jeremy with a smile.

Sheila shot him a look of *you didn't, did you?* But as if on cue, Rudy Wilson yelled from behind his pile of presents, "Hey, look! It's a junior badminton set!" The roaring laughter from the four new friends started in again.

"Look at *this*!" Rudy said when he saw the long, slender package tucked down among the pile of presents. It was wrapped in camouflage paper.

"Open it," said Spencer with a smile.

"Whoa!" Rudy said as he unleashed the stick-soldier from the wrapping. "And look!" he said as he noticed the dog tags hanging on a small silver bead chain that wound around the top of the stick. "These are Army tags!"

"What do they say?" Spencer asked with a grin. Rudy took the small tags in his hand and read the first one. "Rudy's Hiking Stick. Hey! It says my name!"

"What about the other one?" Spencer asked. Rudy turned the second tag around so he could see it.

"If found, please return to Rudy Wilson, 837-6147."

"Well, isn't that clever," Grandpa Theodore said.

"Yeah," Abby chimed in, "Rudy always loses his hiking stick in the woods. That *is* really clever." And all the party guests had to agree. It certainly was.

For the next hour or so, Rudy and his friends played party games in the living room. Some of the guests stuck around to have a second piece of cake-cream *after* presents. By the time the last aunt and uncle left with the final pack of cousins, it was late, and Rudy was exhausted.

Spencer, Jeremy, Sheila, and Claire were in the bonus room off the loft playing Spencer's new video game. Jeremy and Sheila had beat Spencer and Claire the first round, so Team Wilson/Champion was trying to defend its honor and win the next round. Spencer took a break long enough to join his parents, sister, and grandfather when they went in to say goodnight to Rudy and tuck him in.

Rudy thanked Abby for the bike stickers she'd gotten for him, Grandpa Theodore for the fishing lures, and his parents for the new video game. Then he turned to Spencer and said, "And thank you, Spence. I really love the stick and the tags."

"What do you say to trying it out tomorrow on a Sunday hike after church?" his dad asked.

"Sounds good," the Wilsons said in unison. Mrs. Wilson smiled. Family traditions. It's what made a family a family.

CHAPTER TWENTY-TWO

Norman

RUDY WAS UP AT the crack of dawn and was sitting at the kitchen table when his mom came down to start Sunday morning breakfast. Right next to him was his new hiking stick. Normally, their before church breakfast was just quick store-bought cinnamon rolls popped out of a refrigerated tube and baked for ten minutes. But since she had skipped pancake day yesterday due to the birthday party, Rudy's mom decided to kick it up a notch. She outdid her usual with a big country breakfast complete with eggs, bacon, ham, grits, biscuits, fried apples, *and* pancakes! While she fried the bacon and peeled apples, she and Rudy talked about the hike that was planned for later in the day.

"I named my stick Norman," he said to his mom as she tossed the apple peels into the small compost bucket by the sink and handed him a warm biscuit.

She turned to the stick and said, "Are you ready for your first hike, Norman?"

Rudy laughed as his dad entered the room lured in by the smell of the sizzling bacon. "Who's Norman?" he asked, rubbing the back of his neck.

"The stick. Rudy named it Norman."

"Hey," said Spencer coming around the corner and into the kitchen, wiping the sleep out of his eyes, "where's *my* biscuit?"

"Only the early risers get a pre-breakfast sample! Rudy's been up for an hour already. Have a seat and wait for the others to come down."

"I would," Spencer said, "but there's a stick guarding my chair."

"Norman," Spencer's parents and brother corrected in unison.

"Sleep in and you miss a lot around here," his mom said, handing Spencer a tall glass of orange juice. He took it as Grandpa Theodore and Abby trailed into the room.

"What's with the big breakfast, Mom? Did I miss something?" Abby said.

"No, you're just in time, you two. Have a seat. Rudy, will you please say grace?" Mrs. Wilson asked.

Rudy bowed his head and said, "God is

great, God is good, and we thank Him for our food...and for Norman. Amen."

"Who's Norman?" Abby asked as she grabbed her fork to stab a thick piece of country ham. Rudy just shook his head as if the older folks in his family were just too much.

CHAPTER TWENTY-THREE

Home for Christmas

FALL SEEMED TO FLY by and before anyone knew it, the Christmas season was upon them. As usual, Mrs. Wilson was asked to coordinate the Christmas pageant at their small Baptist Church.

"I just can't do it this year," she said to Mr. Wilson at dinner. "The county is mandating the new curriculum and with it, all those reports! I'm just too busy this year. I mean, I could help a bit, but unless someone else steps up as director, I don't think there'll be a program this year."

Claire had joined the Wilson's for dinner that night and was listening to the conversation. "Am I too young to do it?" Claire asked. "You know I love music, and I was student director of the seventh grade play last year. I've got some experience."

"Claire," said Mrs. Wilson, "that would be absolutely wonderful! There's a planning meeting next week. You come to that, and we'll officially name you director of the Benton Baptist Annual Christmas Pageant!"

* * *

Claire worked tirelessly on the pageant in the weeks leading up to the event. She gave Abby the part of Mary. Abby convinced the lady she babysat for to let Claire cast her youngest, six-month old Colton, as baby Jesus. Colton's mom, Mrs. Kelley, was a military wife with a deployed husband and four kids. Two of the children were twins—the kids who had wandered into the yard the day Claire tied the white ribbon on the net. Abby spent much of her time at the Kelley's and was like a regular nanny to the kids. Mrs. Kelley trusted her completely and had no problem with Claire's request.

So, it was agreed that Colton would play baby Jesus under the care of Abby as Mary. Everyone, and especially Claire, wanted smooth sailing during the program and hoped Colton would sleep through his starring role.

Claire was so excited and a little nervous about the production that was to take place during the Christmas Eve service. When Claire asked Spencer if he was coming, he replied, "Are you kidding?

I wouldn't miss it unless the world came to a standstill!"

Well, it wasn't quite the entire world that stood still jeopardizing his chances of seeing the play, but rather a little corner of it. Namely, the Piedmont area of the beautiful state of North Carolina. It rarely snows in North Carolina, except for in the mountains. Since Spencer joined Chad for a December 21 to 23 visit to his cousin's cabin located in the central part of the state, not the mountains, he didn't think much about the winter weather advisory when the alert first went out.

Spencer had heard it all before. Snowfall hysteria, he called it. When flakes did fall in the Piedmont, even a quarter inch, central North Carolinians went crazy with snow fever. Bread, milk, nacho cheese Doritos, and chocolate Moon Pies would fly off grocery store shelves faster than Road Runner high-speed internet.

Kids who didn't own sleds (which happened to be most kids in North Carolina) made them out of laundry baskets, trashcan lids, or anything else they could find to slide like penguins down any snow dusted surface around.

The television meteorologists were just as bad, announcing an impending "snow event" with all the seriousness of a five-alarm fire. And usually nothing happened. A few flakes that might stick to grassy surfaces for an hour or two, and then, gone. All that extra milk and bread for naught.

A dusting at best, thought Spencer after hearing the advisory. *We'll make it home for Christmas Eve, no problem.* When the forecast was updated to include freezing rain followed by six to eight inches of heavy, wet snow, he wasn't so sure. On the morning of December 23 Spencer, Chad, and Chad's cousin Danny woke up in the cabin around eight o'clock to dropping temperatures and ominous skies.

Since the wintry precipitation wasn't expected until late afternoon, Chad's uncle wasn't too concerned, but he asked the boys to start packing the car so they could get an earlier start on their journey home.

Spencer anxiously eyed the gray skies as he made his way out to the car with the first load. Maybe he was feeling some of that snowfall hysteria after all. Walking back to the cabin, he stuffed his hands deep into the pockets of his too-thin hooded sweatshirt and felt the first pellets of sleet sting his face.

Although Chad's uncle owned a getaway cabin near a remote fishing lake, that was where his ruggedness ended. As far as vehicles were concerned, he didn't drive a Jeep or Explorer or even a crossover wanna-be SUV as one might expect of an owner of a rustic fishing cabin. Instead, Spencer and the other three had crammed into a pale blue, two-wheel drive Toyota Prius to head to the remote cabin two days earlier under mild temperatures and dry roads. Now, looking at the icy pellets hitting the windshield, Spencer wished they were in a vehicle that was a little tougher.

Once the snow started falling, it came fast. It was relentless. It was blowing sideways causing near whiteout conditions. The group spent hours crawling along the interstate with other travelers trying to make it to their Christmas holiday destinations. After passing scores of wrecks and stranded vehicles, Chad's uncle pulled into a crowded rest stop off the highway.

"Boys," he said, "I don't think we're going to make it. The radio says the highway patrol has just closed the interstate. That means, the only way home is by way of the backroads. This little hybrid had enough trouble making it on the plowed four-lane. I can't imagine it ever getting us through on the unplowed secondaries. Not to mention, it's getting dark, and the temperatures are still dropping. It might be tomorrow night before these roads are passable. We might have to pull into that motel we passed at the last exit and wait it out."

Spencer let out a long sigh. *Claire,* he thought, *she'll be so disappointed if I miss the pageant.*

Just then, a bright red four-wheel drive truck pulled up alongside the Prius. It had a Red Wagon County Store bumper sticker on its left side. "I know that truck!" Spencer said as he opened his door, uncoiled his legs, and freed himself from the cramped backseat just in time to see Jeremy

Boylan open the passenger side door and jump out without the aid of the chrome running board.

"Hey, Boylan," Spencer said, "I thought you and your dad were heading back from picking up your grandma yesterday."

"Change of plans. Granny's cat escaped, and she wouldn't leave until we found her. You trying to make it back for Christmas Eve?"

"That was the plan," said Chad's uncle who had joined the boys outside the car.

"Not in *that*, you're not," replied Jeremy with a critical glance at the small tires and low clearance on the Prius. "Ain't nobody goin' nowhere for *days* without a four-wheel drive."

Life is a funny thing, thought Spencer. Here he was standing in the middle of a frozen parking lot, facing what was just weeks earlier his longtime enemy. A former enemy who was going in his direction in the only vehicle around that could make the trip. It struck him how just last month he would have had about as much chance getting a ride from Jeremy Boylan as a snowball surviving in a hot frying pan. But everything was different now.

For a fleeting moment an image of an angry Jeremy Boylan walking behind a horse-drawn carriage in pair of baggy pond waders entered Spencer's mind. He would have laughed out loud if it hadn't been for Jeremy interrupting his thought.

After a nod from his dad that said it was okay,

Jeremy said, "Hop in, y'all." Then to his grandmother, he said, "Scoot over, Granny. We got ourselves some stowaways."

The icy sleet turned into thick wet snow with flakes the size of marbles as the brawny red extended cab packed with seven travelers and a cat named Callie headed east toward Benton. Christmas music pounded out of the truck speakers in rhythm with the tires sloshing through thick snow.

Spencer agreed to let Callie ride on his lap the entire way home. Good thing he was a cat person. He didn't care how uncomfortable the ride was. The only thing that mattered was that he made it home. Home for Christmas.

* * *

"Spencer!" Claire shouted as she ran outside to greet him as he trudged up her front walk through snow reaching his knees. Throwing her arms around his neck, she asked, "How in the world did you make it home?"

"You wouldn't believe it if I told you," he said as he scooped her off her feet and carried her inside as the clock turned over a new day. It was 12:01, Christmas Eve.

CHAPTER TWENTY-FOUR

Silent Night, Holy Night

THE CHRISTMAS PAGEANT AT the Benton Baptist Church was one for the memory books. The deacons considered cancelling the service due to the snow, but the young Christmas pageant director wouldn't hear of it. Claire begged the church leaders to keep the doors open despite record snowfall (the official forecast out of Raleigh reported 13.2 inches).

She rounded up every young male in the congregation who had a four-wheel drive truck and put them on parishioner pick up duty. It was a sight to see Ms. Bertha and her sister Ms. Beatrice inch down out of Rusty Miller's 4x4 while hanging on to the driver's burley arm. It took almost an hour to get all the church members packed into the

Silent Night, Holy Night • 131

little sanctuary.

The folks didn't mind the wait a bit. Claire and her sisters had made batch after batch of frosted Christmas cookies and prepared a festive punch that she planned on serving after the performance. To keep everyone occupied while waiting for the last round of trucks to return with their load of Baptists, she broke out the refreshments early, and the folks passed the time fellowshipping and visiting while munching on jolly old Saint Nicks and red nosed Rudolphs.

Just about the time everyone was seated and Ms. Grace began to play the first chords of "Silent Night" on the ancient upright, the sagging power lines outside gave up their fight with the weight of the heavy snow. The lights flickered a few times and then went out, leaving the entire Benton Baptist family in the dark.

"Don't panic," said Brother Phillip Parker as he ran to get the box of candles that the church used for nighttime prayer vigils. In his haste, he tripped over the makeshift manger that Claire had set up as part of the scenery. The ensuing commotion woke baby Jesus, who had been peacefully sleeping in answer to Abby's earlier prayers. That set off the three wise men played by the three Lewis brothers ages 7, 6, and 4. The littlest Lewis started calling out for his mama because he couldn't see her in the darkened sanctuary. His older brothers tried to deliver him to their mom on the first pew, but they got tangled up in their bedsheet robes, and tumbled down like two bowling pins.

Claire just laughed and stepped over the two miniature wise men who were untangling themselves from the heap on the floor and said, "Ladies and gentlemen, let's take a ten minute preshow intermission while Brother Parker helps us light these candles. He is starting with candles at the refreshment table so help yourself to more cookies and punch!"

Cheers rose from the shepherds and angels who were still standing in the dark at the back of the stage. That brought more laughter from Claire and all the adults in the room.

Ten minutes later, the sanctuary was lit with soft candlelight as once again Ms. Grace's "Silent Night" filled the room with calm, joy, and harmony. Abby had even managed to rock baby Jesus back to sleep—to sleep in heavenly peace. Then the narrator, played by Claire's father, began reading, "But the angel said to them, 'Do not be afraid. I bring you good news that will cause great joy for all the people...'"

Seated in the back pew in the sanctuary of the church he'd been a part of since birth, Spencer looked around the room in the soft candlelight. He smiled as he looked to his left to see his former enemy, Jeremy. Spencer had invited Jeremy to attend the service during their harrowing ride home. Jeremy took him up on his invitation and brought Sheila along too. He had even agreed to use his dad's Polaris and join the parishioner pick up duty, gathering up those who lived down roads even too challenging for a 4x4 truck.

Spencer knew a fresh layer of snow was blanketing the ground outside, but inside this place, he was warm, peaceful, and happy. This was his family, his community, and his home. As he looked over at Claire who had just nodded to Ms. Grace to begin "Oh, Holy Night," he saw a tear fall from her eye. He let out a deep sigh of contentment and joined the congregation in singing, "Oh holy night, the stars are brightly shining..."

CHAPTER TWENTY-FIVE

The Quad

AS IF THE INCIDENT at the old Stevenson Place hadn't changed Jeremy enough, the Christmas Eve service at the Benton Baptist Church added to his transformation. Jeremy's family had never attended worship services, so the whole "church family" thing was new to him. In fact, he'd always thought it sounded a little hokey when he'd heard people in the community talk about it. Whether it was seeing people he knew come together to watch their children portray the greatest story ever told—and *really* hearing it for the first time—or whether it was just being a part of helping deliver people to the place through blinding snow on a rugged Polaris, Jeremy felt changed. Renewed. Saved.

* * *

Spencer, Claire, Jeremy, and Sheila had become remarkably close over the winter. Their friendship had blossomed just like the Carolina countryside that was now bursting with spring beauty.

The azaleas were brilliant pink and the Bradford pears full of life. Even beyond the relationship of the four, other friendships were growing. Claire's friends had welcomed Sheila in, as Chad and Spencer's other friends had accepted Jeremy. Not that it didn't take some effort.

Chad and the other boys from BBC cautiously accepted Jeremy into their group. After much persuasion, Claire convinced Ashley, Stephanie, and Jessica to let Sheila into their circle. At first, they had trouble believing she had genuinely changed on the inside as well as the outside. When they got to know her though, they realized that she really had.

Sheila explained it to them one day when they were at the mall food court drinking orange smoothies. "It's not that I underwent a *change* as much as I returned to my true self," she told them.

"How do you mean?" asked Jess.

"Well, I was never comfortable being a 'mean girl' but I did it to get Jeremy's attention. When he changed, it was completely natural and a relief for me to revert to my former self."

It was hard to deny. It wasn't long before their

old ways were altogether forgotten by most of the kids.

Jeremy and Sheila started attending church on Sundays and the youth meetings on Wednesday nights. But mostly the four friends—the Quad as they began referring to themselves—spent their time together at their various homes. Usually that depended on whose house had the best snacks at the time. Spencer's usually did. That actually worked best, because now it was spring, and that meant one thing. Badminton.

"We're gonna teach you two to play badminton, like it or not," said Spencer as they were sitting around the kitchen table eating caramel covered popcorn and drinking root beer. Sheila put her hands up like she'd just been arrested by the Koinonia Festival sheriff at the Great Bandit Round-Up.

"Lead the way," she said. "At least we'll never again get hustled by some closet badminton players."

"I can't argue there," Jeremy added.

Spencer said, "Come on, everyone" and headed for the backyard where four rackets were waiting. There was a white ribbon neatly tied in the far right corner of the black net.

Spencer picked up two of the rackets and tossed them, one at a time, to Sheila and Jeremy. "Racket," he said mimicking a no-nonsense drill sergeant.

Taking his lead, Claire picked up the featherweight cone and said, "Birdie."

"Very funny, you two," Jeremy said. "We did go through weeks of this with Struggs as you might recall."

"Ah, but you didn't get to witness this," Claire said as she watched Boots move into place to watch the game, albeit a doubles match rather than the usual singles. As the Quad began to play, Boots watched the birdie like a hawk.

Jeremy and Sheila showed great promise. Granted, Boots got quite a workout chasing down their out of bounds volleys and dropped serves, but overall, they had a decent game.

The couples met regularly to play throughout the spring. Before long, Sheila and Jeremy had greatly improved their skills. One day after a particularly good match Spencer said, "Hey, you two could probably hold your own against most any couple that dares to challenge you with another homecoming day parade wager."

"Very funny, Spence," Jeremy said as he lobbed a perfect serve over the net to the half of the Quad waiting on the other side.

CHAPTER TWENTY-SIX

Sweet Release

ON THE SATURDAY BEFORE Memorial Day weekend the girls planned to go to the salon and get their nails done. Spencer and Jeremy decided to head out to the reservoir to go fishing. Claire said that the boys could use the Gator, so she dropped the key off at Spencer's before meeting Sheila.

The boys packed some turkey sandwiches, corn chips, chocolate bars, and a few cans of soda as well as their bait and tackle. They parked the Gator at the reservoir gate, took the key, and trekked in with their gear. After they'd been fishing a while Spencer said, "You know, Claire and I were in this very spot when you called that day."

"Oh yeah, *that* day," Jeremy said softly.

"Oh, sorry. I wasn't thinking. Bad memories."

"Well, yes and no," Jeremy said thoughtfully. "Bad because up until that point I had been such a jerk. But good because that day changed all that."

"That's a good way to look at it," Spencer responded and then sat quietly just looking at his bobber still as a statue atop a surface of pure glass.

"You know," Jeremy continued in a low voice, "I guess I needed a drastic event to wake me up. Sort of like needing to hit rock bottom before going up."

Spencer just nodded his head and continued to look out at the water. It was Jeremy's time to talk. That's exactly what Spencer would allow him to do.

"Looking back, I wondered why I didn't just ask myself what it would take for me to change, and then, well..." Jeremy hesitated, trying to put his thoughts into words. After a long moment, he continued, "Just *pretend* that the event or thing happened. It sure would've saved poor Kyle from having to go through that whole ordeal. I mean, he was *scared*. We both were."

Spencer said, "I know what you mean. You always hear of people facing life and death situations and then making that *'Grant this one thing, God, and I swear I'll change'* promise. If they could just imagine what could trigger their change and skip right to the change part, it would save a lot of grief."

"Exactly!" Jeremy said. "Just bat the thing away

before it even happens and move on as a better person."

"Yeah. Goodbye, birdie," Spencer said.

"Huh?" Jeremy said, lost with the badminton analogy.

"Ah, you know, bye-bye. Lights out. It's gone. Like a badminton birdie out of bounds."

"Yes," Jeremy said almost in a whisper, "*just* like that. Goodbye, birdie."

The boys continued to fish until the sun had almost set. They didn't catch much, but the day wasn't about catching anything. It was about release. Sweet, sweet release.

CHAPTER TWENTY-SEVEN

Goodbye Birdie

THE NEXT MORNING AFTER church, the doubles teams planned to meet at the badminton net. Sheila and Jeremy couldn't get enough of the game, and you never had to ask Claire or Spencer twice to play. As they waited for Jeremy, Spencer worked on tightening the net while the girls were chatting and comparing their new manicures.

"Uh, girls, a little help here!" Spencer said.

"Oh! Sorry!" Claire said as they saw the net half caved in on top of Spencer. They each stood by one of the poles, holding the rope as Spencer pulled it tight. They were just about finished when Jeremy appeared. He steered his bike in through the side yard and ditched it by the fence.

"What's that in your hand?" Spencer asked.

"It's a goodbye birdie," said Jeremy as he held up a paper with writing on it. Spencer nodded slowly. He understood completely. The girls, on the other hand, were completely lost.

"It's what?" Sheila asked.

It took a while to explain, but the boys filled the girls in about what transpired at the reservoir. Jeremy summed up the explanation by saying, "To bring closure, I decided I needed to do one final step. I wrote what I needed to change on this paper, and now I'm going to let it go."

"Jeremy," Sheila said quietly, "this is a really special, symbolic event. Do you mind if I video it? I won't if you don't want me to. Just say."

"Yeah," he said, "that might be nice to have." Sheila hit the record button on her phone as Jeremy crumpled the paper into a tiny ball, picked up a birdie and stuffed the note deep inside the hollow core. He walked to the service line and stood still for a moment. Then he raised his racket and dropped the birdie. It hit the racket dead center. With a mixture of finesse and power he hit the birdie, quite literally, out of the park. It nearly reached the creek in the back corner of the Wilson's yard. It was his best serve ever. "Goodbye, birdie," he said softly. And then Sheila hit STOP RECORD.

The Quad stood in silence for a moment just looking toward the creek where the birdie had landed. For whatever reason, Boots, who had been watching the whole event, never moved to chase it. It's almost as if he knew to leave it alone.

"You know, I've been meaning to ask," said Sheila as she broke the silence, "why is that white ribbon tied to the net?"

Spencer smiled a sad smile. "That's a different goodbye, Birdie."

Then Spencer and Claire proceeded to tell their newest friends about their oldest friend, Birdie the cat. As Spencer finished up the story, he looked beyond the birdie, and then beyond his own backyard. He saw one of the Kelley twins playing in her sandbox. Sitting right beside her was Pretty Kitty.

CHAPTER TWENTY-EIGHT

A Plan Takes Shape

IT WAS HARD TO believe that the Koinonia had rolled around again, but sure enough, Memorial Day was upon them and that meant the 37th Koinonia Festival for Benton. Throughout the festival, the Quad reminisced about the events from 35th Festival their sixth grade year and marveled at what a difference the time had made. There was no dunk tank episode or egg yolk drama this year, but it was a great day of real koinonia with true friends.

After the long day, the four sat on a blanket waiting for the fireworks to begin. "You know," Jeremy said, "I can't imagine how my life would be if I hadn't changed. I wouldn't be here with you now. I'd still be looking for a fight."

"Sheila's hair would still be jet-black," Claire interjected with a smile. They all laughed at the memory of it all.

"No, but seriously," Jeremy continued, "I wonder how many other people out there could learn from my mistakes."

"I bet you're right," said Spencer. And that got him thinking. Just then, the sky exploded into a huge ball of brilliant red, white, and blue sparkles. The crowd around them made sounds of amazement as one spectacular display after another lit the sky.

As the fireworks continued, a plan began to take shape in Spencer's mind. By the time the grand finale rolled around, the plan was as good as done.

CHAPTER TWENTY-NINE

A Better Benton

THE END OF MEMORIAL Day weekend meant one thing for the students in the sixth and seventh grades at BMS. There were only two more weeks of school. It meant an altogether different thing for the eighth graders. There were only two more weeks until their graduation projects were due. Yes, another great tradition at Benton Middle. Each eighth grader—or team of eighth graders if they decided to work together—had to complete their *Make Benton a Better Place* project by the final week of school.

The parameters were fairly loose. The project simply had to demonstrate some initiative or act that would contribute to the betterment of the community. Most kids did your basic litter pick up day, started a recycling or compost effort, or made a few token visits to the local nursing home. The parents, teachers, and a few community members came to watch the project presentations. It was essentially the eighth grade graduation ceremony. Naturally, the Quad had teamed up and was all set to present their report on their volunteer work at the local animal shelter.

They had photos of themselves cleaning out the dog cages, scooping food into cat feeding bowls, and helping distribute pet adoption flyers throughout the community. Done. Box checked. High school here we come.

All that changed in Spencer's mind as he sat under the Benton night sky, watching fireworks to celebrate the town's love and fellowship. It all changed because the problem was, not everyone was loveable. For example, take Jeremy less than one year ago. But he overcame, and Spencer was convinced that others could learn from Jeremy's story. They just needed a way to get the message out.

* * *

Most of the parishioners struggled to stay awake during the sermon at church the next morning. The festivities the day before and the late night due to the closing fireworks had taken their toll. But good Baptists don't miss church just because they had a little too much koinonia the day before, so the pews were packed.

After the four friends had squeezed into their seats, Spencer scrawled a note on his bulletin and passed it down the line:

> CAN YOU MEET ME AT THE WILLOW AT 2:00 TODAY?
>
> J: ☐ Y ☐ N
> S: ☐ Y ☐ N
> C: ☐ Y ☐ N

A moment later the note made its way back to Spencer at the end of the row. Y was checked next to each initial. Spencer folded the bulletin and stuck it in the pew rack in front of him like an airline passenger tucking a magazine in the seatback pocket. He then turned to page 129 in his hymnal, as instructed by the music director, and began singing, "Come Thou Fount of Every Blessing."

* * *

Jeremy arrived first and sat on the bench under Willodean to wait for the others. He looked up at the massive branches and said right out loud, "Sorry, Willodean. I shouldn't have stolen your ribbons that day. I'm not the same person I was then."

"No, you're not," Spencer said as he walked up behind Jeremy.

"Oh, you heard that," Jeremy said. "Now I feel *really* stupid for getting caught talking to a tree."

"She's not just tree," Spencer said. "She's really more like a member of the family, but that's beside the point."

Just then, the girls arrived. As they sat on the grass by the bench, Claire said, "What's up?"

"I've got an idea," Spencer began, "for our *Better Benton* project."

"What do you mean?" Sheila asked. "We're finished with that. We've just got to add a few more captions to the poster board, and we're done."

"Yeah, well, about that. . ." Spencer said. The three friends sent him a skeptical look. They knew something was coming. Scrapping what they had and starting over is what they suspected.

"The goal of the project is to better the community, right?" Spencer asked, sounding more like a teacher than an eighth grader.

"Ours betters the community," Jeremy retorted.

"Yes, it does," Spencer said. "Rescuing dogs and cats is very important. Just ask Mittens and Boots."

"I hear a *but* coming," Sheila said flatly.

"Yeah," Spencer continued, "but we've got a message that can really make an impact. One that can *really* change people for the better. It's right there in Sheila's phone." Spencer pointed to the iPhone in a pink glitter phone case that Sheila was holding.

"Huh?" the other three said in perfect unison. Spencer then spent the next thirty-five minutes explaining his plan.

"Jeremy said that he wished waking up and changing his ways hadn't taken Kyle having to go through the terrifying event at the Stevenson place."

"True," Jeremy agreed.

"So, our presentation could be called *What Would It Take for You to Change?* and we show the goodbye, birdie video with a voice-over of us explaining the concept—making a life change *before* hitting rock bottom to save everyone involved a lot of pain."

"Hmm," Claire said, trying to make sense of the idea. "So that's it? We just show the video? What would we do after that?"

Spencer said, "I'm glad you asked! We'd host a Goodbye Birdie Day!"

Spencer said that as if it explained everything.

"I'm not sure I'm following," Sheila said.

Spencer said, "Follow me on this. After showing the video, we'd ask the audience to think about any changes needed in their lives. Be kinder to their parents, stop picking on a younger sibling or classmate, whatever it might be. Then maybe we'd pass out pieces of paper, just like the one Jeremy had in the video. They could think about it as bypassing the painful life-changing event and skipping right to the change part. They'd write the thing they want to change on the paper.

"Then we'd announce the time and date for our Goodbye Birdie Day for those who wanted to come by and actually bat their issue away," Spencer said, air quoting "bat."

"How would the event work?" Claire asked.

"We could have it at Lake Side," Spencer answered. "Set up the net, bring plenty of rackets, and a supply of "goodbye birdies"—sort of make a ceremony out of it."

"Hmm," Claire said again, nodding her head slowly.

"What do you think? Other questions?" Spencer asked, sounding again like a teacher.

"Would everyone in the audience have to write something on their paper after we show the video?" asked Sheila.

"Nope," Spencer said, "it's strictly voluntary. Most might though after seeing how impactful it was for Jeremy. In fact, Jeremy, maybe we can record a testimonial from you and add it to the video. You know, have you sort of recap the whole story before we show the scene at the net."

"Ah, yeah," Jeremy said hesitantly, "but my parents don't even know the whole story. They saw a change in me, sure, and were really happy about it. But they never knew why. Kyle agreed not to tell them, so we never did."

"Well, maybe it's time to come totally clean.

Like you said, they were really happy to see the change in you."

Jeremy sat quiet for a moment. "I've always felt bad about asking Kyle to keep the secret. Maybe it *is* time. Okay. I'll do it," he said, nodding his head firmly.

"I have another question," Sheila piped in.

"Yes?" Teacher Spencer responded.

"What if we set up the whole event at Lake Side and nobody shows?"

"That's a real possibility," Spencer affirmed. "But if just *one* person shows up and stuffs their note down inside a birdie and bats the bad out of their life, I'd say it'd be worth it. I'd say it would go a long way toward making Benton a better place."

And then Spencer stuck his fist out into the center of the circle that the friends had made on the ground under Willodean. One by one, Claire, Sheila, then Jeremy reached out and the four fists bumped. The plan was a go.

CHAPTER THIRTY

What Would it Take?

YOU COULD HAVE HEARD a pin drop in the gymnasium of Benton Middle School after the *What Would It Take for You to Change?* project team finished their presentation. The sound of Jeremy's soft voice saying, "Goodbye, birdie" lingered even after the video clip finished playing.

Spencer glanced over at Jeremy's parents sitting on the old wooden bleachers. Jeremy's mom was wiping away tears while she watched her son openly and honestly admit his bullying ways to his entire school community. It was no secret to her. She'd witnessed him bully his own little brother on more than one occasion.

"Well, now," the principal said as she stepped back to the podium. "That was," she paused for the right word, "powerful. I hope that many of you will consider joining these thoughtful young people at Lake Side Park next Saturday morning at ten for their event. And now, we'll hear from Angela Haines and Aubrey Dillon with *Baking Sunshine for the Shut-Ins*."

The audience clapped politely and gave the pair their attention, but truth be told, nobody could stop thinking about the image of that birdie flying through the air.

* * *

The four friends woke early on the day of their event and met up in Spencer's driveway to load the net and rackets in the Gator just as the morning sun was burning the last of the dew off the grass.

"Why's there a ribbon on Willodean?" asked Sheila, "Is it somebody's birthday?"

"Nope," Spencer said. "Ribbons go up for all kinds of significant events in the family. Guess Mom thought this was a special enough day to warrant a ribbon."

As if on cue, Mrs. Wilson emerged from the house with several large trays of cookies and a bright orange Gatorade sports jug she used when bringing refreshments to Rudy's soccer games.

"I hope you don't mind. I thought it might be nice to serve some refreshments at your event. Do you have room for these?"

"Sure, Mom, thanks," Spencer said, taking the trays from her and setting them in the cargo area of the Gator, "but we're not sure if anyone will even show up. There's a lot of cookies here."

"No worries," she said. "We can give them to the *Sunshine for Shut-Ins* girls if nobody shows."

The Quad smiled at Mrs. Wilson's playful reference to their classmates' nursing home project.

"Hey, thanks for the ribbon, Mrs. Wilson," Jeremy said, pointing at Willodean. "I promise not to destroy this one."

"That was *you?*" she said with a look of surprise.

"Fraid so. This has been the week to come clean, so yeah, and I am truly sorry 'bout that, Mrs. Wilson."

He hopped in the Gator with his three friends, and they slowly backed down the drive and onto Cardinal Lane.

CHAPTER THIRTY-ONE

Lake Side

CLAIRE STEERED THE DEERE through country paths and trails until they came out along the back side of Lake Side Park. It was still early, well over an hour before the ten o'clock event was to start.

Jeremy was a little quiet as Claire maneuvered around the lake. The memory of him snatching the keychain off Spencer's backpack flooded his mind. Not that he hadn't apologized a hundred times for that by now, especially after hearing the full story about Birdie, but it didn't lessen the pain of the memory.

As if reading his mind, Spencer said, "You gotta let that go, Jeremy. See, no loss, no foul. It's still here." He shifted his backpack a bit and then tugged at the cat beanbag keychain that Claire had twice now reattached to the pack. Jeremy just nodded, grateful for the forgiveness extended by his new best friend.

They busied themselves setting up the poles, stringing the net, and laying the rackets out on the soft grass. Although they knew nobody would be playing an actual game—and therefore need the net—they set it up anyway to recreate the original scene. Claire had brought a stack of extra papers and a few pens in case somebody wanted to participate but didn't bring their paper from the graduation ceremony held at the school. She set those on the ground in a pile by the rackets.

Sheila added a sheet that she'd created to ask each participant to give or decline their permission to have their birdie serve videotaped by Sheila McCalister. Sheila thought that maybe somebody would want a recording of their pledge to look at later. The girls then set up the cookies, drink cooler, napkins, and cups on a nearby picnic table.

Tasks completed, the four of them sat down in the quiet, empty park to wait. The silence was almost awkward.

"I think I'll have a cookie and some lemonade while I wait," said Spencer, getting up abruptly.

"Good idea," Claire said, following behind. They each made their way to the picnic table and grabbed a paper cup. They filled their cups and looked over the cookie selection. Claire picked an oatmeal raisin, Spencer a snickerdoodle, and Jeremy and Sheila both selected chocolate chip. As they were walking back to the net, they saw a small group heading their way across the park. Each person was carrying a piece of paper.

By ten o'clock, there were easily two hundred people gathered around the pro badminton net. Students were there. Teachers were there. The principal was there. Parents and siblings—theirs included—were there. Dr. Munch showed up specifically to pitch in with anything that needed to be done. He told his former student, Claire, how proud of her he was for being part of the team that planned such a meaningful, real-world learning event.

Yes, it seemed as if the whole town was turning out! Even a reporter from the local newspaper was spotted in the back of the crowd capturing the event with his high-powered Nikon.

What really amazed the Quad though was that it wasn't just their classmates who were lining up to bat away their crumpled notes. There were older *and* younger people who had an issue they wanted to resolve. Nobody seemed embarrassed to step up and admit they had something they wanted to change.

Some teachers had lined up, some parents, the elementary school principal, the Benton mayor, and even a few local preachers. Spencer and Claire also noticed someone who looked a lot like one of the cat catchers they'd met out at the old church. Nobody really knew for sure how the word about the Goodbye Birdie event spread, but it *was* a small town. It doesn't take long after somebody sneezes in Benton for the whole town to know they have a cold.

The team stayed busy all morning. To Sheila's surprise, everyone checked the *yes* box on the form to have their serve recorded. Claire and Jeremy helped people with crumpling their papers and shoving them down inside the goodbye birdies.

Rudy, Kyle, and some of their friends were tasked with retrieving the birdies and returning them to the servers so that they could privately discard their crumpled notes if they wished. Spencer gave pointers on how to deliver a good, solid serve. Not everyone caught on. Some dropped their birdies or sent the thing a mere two inches in front of them rather than over the net or out of the park. For some, it looked like the famous Claire and Spencer Badminton Hustle.

But that was okay. It relieved some of the nervous tension at the solemn moment. Some of the people were grappling with serious personal struggles. For others, it was lighter. Some of the little kids that joined in said that they'd written on their papers a pledge not to argue about eating their vegetables at dinner or fuss about picking up all of their toys when asked. That was okay too. It had become a personal event for each individual there. It was about whatever that person needed—to grow, or change, or become better. Making a better Benton.

CHAPTER THIRTY-TWO

The News Spreads

ADAM ADAMS, YES THAT really is his name, wrote articles for the *Benton Chronicle*. The paper comes out weekly, so it wasn't until the Saturday after the Goodbye Birdie event took place that Adam's article appeared. Spencer's mom cut out the article, framed it using an extra photo frame she scrounged, and hung it on the stairway wall.

The event had generated a lot of talk in the town, but like everything, the dust had begun to settle a bit. Spencer was sitting at the kitchen table eating peanut butter and banana on toast—one of his all-time favorites. Just as he was about to finish the last bite, his phone chirped to indicate an incoming text.

Turn on the TV. Channel 11.

He sent back a thumbs up and grabbed the remote. As he landed on the channel, he heard the newscaster from the Raleigh station say, "And, as we said before the break, we finish our broadcast this evening with a heart-warming story out of Benton."

"Benton!" Spencer repeated as he called his family members to the room. They rushed in as the screen showed video of the scene at Lake Side Park with the news anchor narrating the highlights of the day.

"How'd they get that video?" Spencer mused. "It doesn't look like any Sheila took."

"I'm guessing the local reporter grabbed some video in addition to the stills he took for the paper. He must have sent it to the station in Raleigh," Mrs. Wilson said.

"Well I'll be darned," Grandpa Theodore said. "You put Benton on the map, son."

Just as the frame cut out, Spencer caught sight of the white ribbon that was tied at the corner of the net. *Why, hello, Birdie*, he said to himself. *You made the big city news.*

CHAPTER THIRTY-THREE

As Luck Would Have It

AS LUCK WOULD HAVE it, not only did local area viewers see the newscast that evening but some visitors did too. One of those visitors happened to be twenty-three-year-old Andrew Young. He caught the story while watching television in his hotel room in Durham.

"Wow," said Andrew when he saw the story, "that's pretty cool." And that got him thinking.

With the help of a little internet searching, Andrew was able to reach the principal at Benton Middle. He explained who he was and why he wanted to set up a meeting with her and the Wilsons, Champions, Boylans, and McCalisters. She immediately called Mrs. Wilson to arrange the meeting.

"Andrew Young." Spencer said to Jeremy when they found out about the meeting. "Do you know who that is?"

"Can't say that I do," Jeremy said.

"Andrew Young is *Smash*!" said Spencer. "He's one of the, if not *the*, all-time best players in the World Professional Badminton League—the PBL. I've followed him my whole life! He lives in California, but he's in North Carolina for an East Coast PBL meeting my dad said."

"Well, why does he want to meet with us?" Jeremy asked.

"I have no idea," said Spencer, "but I guess we'll find out soon. The meeting is tomorrow night!"

The next evening, to Spencer's astonishment, his idol, Smash Young was sitting in *his* living room with his family, his principal, and his three best friends in the world.

It took a little time to work out the details, but Smash had proposed holding another Goodbye Birdie event. This time on national television after one of the televised games in the PBL. The league had offered to pay for the four friends and their immediate family members to fly to San Diego, California, to attend the event. Spencer, upon hearing that, quickly clarified that Grandpa Theodore would be counted as immediate.

"Absolutely!" Smash said as he stuck his fist out for a bump with Grandpa, who was sitting on the couch.

Grandpa Theodore, who wasn't quite with it when it came to the younger generation, looked at the fist confused. He held out a flat hand to shake, so Smash quickly switched gears and gave Grandpa a good old-fashioned handshake.

The parents of the four spent the next weeks communicating with Smash and the Professional Badminton League to work out all the details of the event and the trip. They would fly out very early the morning of the event, making it to California in plenty of time to check into their hotel and relax a bit before heading to the arena to set up for the evening event. PBL was arranging their stay at a four star hotel. They would have the whole next day to explore the sights and then head back the following morning.

Spencer, Claire, Jeremy, and Sheila were excited beyond measure. The plan was to replicate, on a national scale, the event that was held at Lake Side. It would, of course, begin with the video. Jeremy was still amazed at how much interest that video had generated.

Somebody, he never determined who, posted it on the web a few days after the event at Lake Side. Since that time, it had received over 3,200 views and had garnered over 100 comments from people pledging to turn over a new leaf. And that was before the PBL event. He imagined those numbers might skyrocket after the national exposure.

Recognition of the four would be fast-tracked

too, as each of them was scheduled to play a significant part in the event. They had been asked to speak as well as facilitate the event by helping the attendees from across the nation who were slated to participate.

Jeremy was unbelievably nervous about sharing his story on national TV, but his friends assured him he'd do an amazing job. The four knew the impact that the final words in the video had on the *small* crowd gathered in the BMS auditorium. It was almost impossible to fathom how impactful Jeremy's soft-spoken, "goodbye, birdie" would be as it hung in the air of the gigantic indoor sports arena when the video faded out. They'd know soon enough. The trip would be here before they knew it. In no time, they'd be boarding a big bird—of sorts—and soaring through the sky heading straight toward sunny California.

CHAPTER THIRTY-FOUR

A Storm Approaches

EVERYONE WHO LIVES ON the East Coast knows that the Atlantic Coast hurricane season runs from June to November. Residents of Benton, North Carolina—the tiny town with a population of 950 located one hundred twenty miles from the coast—were no exception. They'd had their share of powerful storms come through their town causing massive flooding, severe wind damage, and wide-spread power outages. From Hazel in 1954 to Bertha and Fran in 1996, the townspeople in Benton were not exempt from danger even though they lived over a hundred miles inland.

As the teachers at Benton Middle School explained to their students during Hurricane Awareness Week, the massive storms, such as

Florence and Michael in 2018, could be over four hundred miles across and pack violent winds in excess of 155 miles per hour. With a storm that size, it was possible that the very eye could cut through the center of their inland town like a kitchen knife through a brick of softened cream cheese. Residents knew to take hurricane warnings seriously and prepare for the worst. Flashlights, extra batteries, portable radios, and water were staples in the hurricane preparedness kits that most families kept close by when storms threatened.

* * *

Claire was not thinking about hurricanes that morning when she suggested that she and Sheila go shopping for new clothes.

"We're going to be on *national* TV in four days," Sheila said as she poured through the racks of cute blouses, jackets, and scarfs. "We need to find something soon!" Their baskets were full to the brim when they wheeled them to the fitting rooms.

It took forty-five minutes for them to try on all their selections, but each had settled on the perfect outfit for their television debut. Claire opted for a cobalt blue blouse made of wispy fabric. It flared out at the bottom with an uneven edge that gave it unique style. She planned to wear a white denim jacket with the sleeves rolled up to about three quarters length over the blouse. To complete the outfit, she selected a pair of dark blue jeans that fit more like leggings.

"Oh! I love it, Claire!" Sheila said as her friend stepped out of the dressing room.

Sheila was standing in front of the three-way mirror at the end of dressing rooms analyzing her choice. She picked a lime green shirt made of a soft fabric that had a crinkle look to it. It had two ribbons that hung down from either side of the three decorative buttons at the top. The ribbons ended in smooth tassels that matched the lime green fabric. She'd decided on a pair of white tapered jeans similar to Claire's dark jeans.

"What do you think?" Sheila said, holding her hands out in a pose.

"Yep," Claire said, "get it!" In a few minutes, the girls emerged from their dressing rooms, returned the items they weren't purchasing to the fitting room clerk, and tossed their selections in their baskets.

"Now, to the shoes," Sheila said as they wheeled their carts toward the back of the store to peruse the shoe section. When they passed Electronics, Claire paused at the massive wall of televisions, showing pictures but no sound. They were all showing the same channel. It happened to be the news. The meteorologist was standing in front of a huge map of the U.S. and areas south of it in the Atlantic Ocean. She pointed to a big blob of white and gray swirls that were over some small islands. The closed caption at the bottom of the screen read,

> "THIS COULD BE THE FIRST NAMED STORM TO REACH THE U.S. THIS SEASON, BUT IT'S TOO EARLY TO TELL THE TRACK IT WILL TAKE AS IT'S STILL AT LEAST THREE DAYS OUT."

Claire and Sheila headed on to the shoe department without another thought about the weather.

* * *

When the day before the scheduled flight arrived, Spencer began his packing. He wasn't like the girls who had been packing for the last several days. As he was tucking another stack of clothes into his suitcase, he paused again to listen to the television. The chief meteorologist on the local station was reporting on the latest track of an active hurricane.

"Alice, the first named storm of the season, has just been upgraded from a Category 1 to a Cat 3 hurricane. Storm Tracker indicates that the storm is expected to make landfall near Wilmington sometime in the overnight hours. Alice is expected to be a Category 4 storm by the time it makes landfall, packing damaging winds in excess of 125 miles per hour. Residents from Wilmington to towns as far inland as Raleigh, Durham, and Chapel Hill are urged to take necessary precautions. Stay tuned to WRAL for further updates. We now return to regularly scheduled broadcasting," said the announcer.

Tomorrow? Our flight is tomorrow. What does this storm mean for us since we are supposed to fly out of Raleigh-Durham airport? Spencer wondered.

Spencer dismissed the notion that this storm could impact them taking off for their trip, so ignoring the ominous forecast, he returned to his packing. He glanced up as his dad knocked, then entered his bedroom.

"You heard the weather report?" his dad said softly.

"Dad, what are you saying? We're still going aren't we?" Spencer asked, trying to process the seriousness of the forecast.

His dad looked down at the open suitcase. He looked at the badminton racket that was sticking out of Spencer's backpack beside the suitcase. It struck him how much bigger this racket was than the child-sized one that came with the first badminton set Spencer had gotten on his eighth birthday. He repeated in his mind the phrase his wife always said, *Where does the time go?* He laid his hand on Spencer's shoulder and said, "I'm sorry, son."

The biggest thing that had ever happened to

him was just a day away, and it was being ruined by a storm named Alice.

As if to add insult to Spencer's grief, the television meteorologist once again interrupted regular programming and announced, "The latest storm track now shows Hurricane Alice making landfall just north of Wilmington, North Carolina, between midnight and two a.m. Maximum sustained winds are at 125 miles per hour with gusts as high as 145 miles per hour reported in some areas.

"Major coastal flooding and inland flooding along the path of the storm for the areas of Raleigh, Garner, and Durham are expected. Residents in the path of the storm who live in flood-prone areas are urged to seek higher ground in local storm shelters immediately. We'll bring you the latest updates as they become available."

"It's bad, Spencer," said his dad. "Businesses all over the area are closing early today and many have already announced closings for tomorrow."

"Well," Spencer said desperately, "check with the airlines! Maybe we can get on a plane tonight and get ahead of the storm."

"I already did. Some flights are already cancelled, and the ones that *are* going are full. Not a seat left. Seems like everybody had that idea to get a jump on the storm."

"This is unbelievable," Spencer said, fighting back a tear.

"There's no way we can make it to San Diego. I'm sorry, Spence."

When his dad left the room, Spencer grabbed his phone and created a group text. To all he typed: Have you heard? My dad says there's no way we're going. This is awful!!!!

In seconds,

CLAIRE: IKR? Devastated. :(

SHEILA: NOOOOOOOO!!!!

JEREMY:
The worst. Did anyone check if there's a way to go tonight?

SPENCER:
My dad checked. Nothing. He just called Smash. It's official.
Trip is off.

CHAPTER THIRTY-FIVE

Hold on Tight

IT BROKE HIS MOM'S heart to see Spencer so down. Actually, Rudy and Abby were moping around too. They were missing out on a trip to California as well. She was sure Spencer's friends and their families were just as deflated. She decided it might cheer everybody up to be together at least for a little while before the storm kicked into full gear.

She called and invited the Champions, Boylans, and Ms. McCalister (Sheila's parents were divorced, and she lived with her mom) over for a Southern meal of fried chicken, boiled potatoes, hush puppies, slaw, fried okra, and homemade banana pudding. "It might be a while until we can eat like this again if the power cuts off. We should enjoy it while we can," she said.

After dinner, the families gathered in the living room. Claire suggested that they pull up the *Goodbye Birdie* video that had been posted and look through some of the comments. Spencer hooked up his laptop to the TV mounted above the fireplace so they all could see.

As they scrolled through the now almost 200 comments, Spencer's mom said, "I'm inspired by reading them."

They all agreed that it had sparked a good thing, and they were happy to see that it had helped so many people. Breaking the moment, a huge wind gust rattled the window, almost as if to say, "Party's over."

"Gusts already!" Ms. McCalister said.

"It's the outer bands reaching us," said Mr. Boylan.

Mrs. Champion said, "I guess we should all get back home before the winds really kick up."

The adults got up and thanked the Wilsons for a lovely dinner and evening. The kids had a big, sad group hug, coming to final terms that their trip was, well, for lack of a better term—goodbye, birdie.

It didn't take long after the guests left before the winds grew fiercer and the rain started. The gusts were coming more frequently and with increasing intensity. Before heading for bed, Spencer grabbed his laptop so that he could disconnect the cord that ran from the computer to the large screen.

His mom said, "That was a nice way to do that, Spencer. To project it so that we could all see."

"That's it!" Spencer said, and his fingers danced across his keyboard clicking buttons until a flashing lightning bolt icon appeared on the large screen in front of them. In a few seconds, Claire's face filled the screen.

"Hey," she said. "Why are you calling me on MeetXTRA?"

"I'm testing something. I've got you projected on the large screen," he said as he was zooming in and out on the picture.

"Oh, hi!" she said to all the Wilsons who had wandered back into the living room. "I think I know what you're thinking, Spence. But what if the power goes out? We won't be able to connect to the arena in San Diego."

"Power out?" Mr. Wilson said, looking at Claire on the large screen, "No worries there. I've got a 3,200-watt generator just waiting to power up!"

Spencer asked Claire to text the others. "Tell Jeremy he might not be off the hook for that speech," he said. "We may still be going to California—virtually, that is."

Since it was three hours earlier in California than in North Carolina, Smash Young hadn't even eaten dinner yet when Spencer called. When Spencer pitched the idea of connecting virtually to the event scheduled for the following evening, Smash thought it was a great suggestion. Before

Smash hung up, he said, "Don't you worry. While you sleep tonight, we'll put together the technology needed to bring the Goodbye Birdie kids virtually from Benton to San Diego, right through the eye of a hurricane."

As Spencer hung up, the power flickered twice inside the Wilson home, and then it cut off completely.

"I guess that means lights out," Spencer's mom said.

They all laughed, and then the six Wilsons made their way through the dark toward their safe, cozy beds.

As Spencer ascended the stairs with his family beside him, he turned and looked back down the stairs and out the front window. In a voice so low he wasn't sure he could be heard over the howling winds outside he said, "Night, Willodean. Hold on tight."

The winds that night were like nothing Spencer had ever seen or heard before. He watched horrified out the window as tall Carolina pines swayed to and fro like the giant tube-man dancers outside used car dealerships. Rain fell in sideways sheets, battering the windows until the panes shook. Even items that had been tied down like lawn furniture and trashcan lids were tossed about like unwanted possessions. Alice was upon them, and she'd come in with a vengeance.

CHAPTER THIRTY-SIX

Cleanup

THE MORNING AFTER A major storm is always a little unnerving. It isn't until the sun fully rises that residents can take in the damage and devastation that the winds and rain left behind in their wake. Alice proved to be historic in terms of what she left for Benton residents.

Roads everywhere were impassable due to flooding and downed powerlines. Trees, snapped like toothpicks, were creating huge hazards for residents trying to venture out and survey the damages. Spencer woke early to the sounds of chainsaws that could be heard throughout the neighborhoods as homeowners began the work of storm cleanup.

He went to his closet to grab a sweatshirt. Out

of habit, he flipped the light switch. Nothing. *Of course. Power still out.* In looking out his window and seeing the devastation, Spencer understood. *Yep. Nobody flying out of RDU today, that's for sure.*

Rudy woke not long after Spencer and headed down to the kitchen with Norman. His parents and Grandpa Theodore were sitting at the table in the darkened room drinking lukewarm coffee out of a thermos filled the night before. The adults had been through enough hurricanes to know that coffee from a thermos, even made the night before the power goes out, is better than no coffee at all. Spencer and Abby were eating cold Pop Tarts.

"We were supposed to go to California today," Rudy said, as if announcing something the rest of them didn't know. Then he looked out the kitchen window at a huge oak tree laying diagonally across the Wilson's driveway, extending all the way to the Champion's front yard. "We're not going anywhere," he declared, again as if all of his family members had somehow missed the giant storm that swept through the state at full force.

It was all hands on deck for Operation Alice Cleanup. Since the event in California didn't start until seven p.m. Pacific Time, that meant it wasn't showtime for them until ten p.m. Eastern. That gave them plenty of time to help their families with storm cleanup *and* do one last run-through of their speeches and comments to their virtual audience.

As Spencer filled his third wheel barrel with downed tree limbs, he was sort of wishing he didn't have the whole day ahead of him free to help. He generally didn't mind helping his dad with yardwork though, so he carried on with a smile. He pushed his wheel barrel over to Willodean to start gathering her downed limbs. Mixed in with the thin branches and wispy leaves that she had lost during the storm were shreds of red ribbon from around her trunk.

Spencer smiled thinking of the ribbon on the willow to announce his special event. Appearing on national TV was not your ordinary, everyday thing. Of course, it warranted a ribbon! His dad came up behind him and said, "The old girl faired pretty well," pointing a mud-covered work glove at the tree.

Spencer just nodded. He couldn't imagine how devastating it would be for the family if anything happened to the old willow. He scooped up the small branches and scraps of ribbon and tossed them in the wheel barrel. Just then he saw Claire across the street. She was helping Mrs. Champion pick up the flowerpots that had been toppled during the night.

Claire hollered, "See you later this afternoon!"

Rudy bounded up with Norman. He raised the stick and waved at Claire.

"Nice stick!" she yelled.

"Norman," Rudy corrected, and then turned

around with his soldier to inspect some other area of the one-acre yard.

About mid-afternoon the four gathered on Spencer's back patio and connected to Smash on Spencer's laptop. Smash agreed to help them with their run-through and to check that all the technology was working to bring them virtually onto the jumbotron in the arena. In a few seconds, Smash's face with his scruffy goatee filled the screen. It was still early for him. He had a rustic glazed porcelain coffee cup in his hand. A true hippie.

"Good morning, my friends," Smash said as he made a peace sign with his fingers. "How'd you fare last night?"

"Not too good, but a mass cleanup has been underway all morning. We'll get there. The power is still out, but we're plugged into Dad's generator."

"Cool beans," Smash responded.

As they ran through the order of events in the program, Spencer mentioned to Smash that a few of their friends who had missed the Lake Side event asked if their papers could be taken to California and ceremoniously batted away by the Benton team on their behalf.

"I guess now that we're participating through live stream, we won't do that part."

"Not necessarily, bro," Smash said. "I can see your whole back yard from the feed right now—are you sitting outside or something?"

"Yeah," Spencer said. "We're sitting on the

back patio. Dad has this whole outdoor living area here with his grill and a firepit."

"Does it have lights? Would it light part of the backyard?"

"It sure does and I think it will!" Claire interjected.

"Sweet," Smash said, "Can you contact your friends who gave you their papers? Would they agree to come join the broadcast and do their own serves using your net? Get some coast-to-coast action going?"

Sheila interjected, "I'm sure they would!"

The run-through lasted another half hour. Smash said that Jeremy's speech was "right on," which made Jeremy feel much better about the whole thing.

"It's gonna be great. We'll see you in a few hours," Smash said. Then he added, "Goodbye, Birdies." The screen went blank as the Quad chuckled at the humor of their famous new friend.

CHAPTER THIRTY-SEVEN

Birdie Craze

WHEN THE PBL TECHNOLOGY team in California connected with the Benton Birdies in North Carolina before the event was to begin, the Quad was astounded at what they saw on their screen. The auditorium was huge and scores of people were running around taking care of last minute details. They commented to each other that it was almost like seeing time-lapse footage as they watched the auditorium fill with fans.

A sizable group of friends and relatives, including the classmates who were slated to bat their birdies from Spencer's backyard, showed up to view the streaming event with the Quad and their families. As predicted, Jeremy's speech thoroughly captivated the audience. The applause was deafening even through the audio stream. Also as predicted, the video completely mesmerized the fans as they watched the birdie fly through the Carolina sky. All agreed that Smash's idea for coast-to-coast action of birdies being batted both live in the arena and virtually on the jumbotron was a smashing success, pun intended!

By the time the event ended it was after one a.m. Eastern time, but the Benton Birdies and their families were too wired to sleep. Mr. Wilson threw some logs in the fire pit and the group roasted marshmallows and made S'mores. As they sat around the fire watching the last log burn down to gray coals, they agreed it had been quite a day.

The PBL announced afterwards that the Birdie event captured their largest viewing audience ever recorded. It seemed that the hype generated by the Benton Birdies—a name that was now commonly associated with the four—had put badminton on the road to becoming a mainstream sport. The Birdie craze that had started as an eighth grade graduation project had done much more than make a better Benton. It was making a better world. The number of views on the original video posted totaled now in the millions from all over the world.

All kinds of strange things started to happen. Sports stores all over the country were running out of stock on anything associated with badminton. The factories that made birdies reported they had to up their production to meet demand. The Quad had heard that school systems, churches, and counseling centers all over the country were ordering bulk quantities of badminton supplies for Goodbye Birdie events that were being planned. There were even souvenirs and little badminton knickknacks that had popped up all over. Smash had his lawyers draw up a contract to protect the use of the Benton Birdies' likenesses and the Birdie brand.

That meant actual *income* for the four kids from Benton, who one day made a twenty-seven second video of a former bully batting a birdie over a net with a white ribbon tied on the corner. How much money? They weren't really sure.

Smash said he'd seen all too often young kids go off the deep end where money was involved. Their parents couldn't have agreed more, so his lawyer drew up four trusts that were signed by the parents of each child. The kids would see how much they had received when they turned twenty-one, but for now, they were just normal kids from Benton. Except they weren't exactly normal anymore. They began receiving invitations from the community to speak, present, talk to groups, and even coach badminton.

They had spent the morning at Lake Side Park coaching the eight- to ten-year-old *Strings*, a team from the county summer rec league that had sprung up overnight. Since both Rudy and Kyle were on the team and the Quad didn't have a lot of pressing plans for the summer, they couldn't say no.

As they pulled the Gator into Spencer's driveway after a long morning of coaching, they noticed three ribbons tied neatly around Willodean. One red. One white. One blue. They piled in through the front door of the Wilson home and Claire, Sheila, and Jeremy plopped down at the kitchen table. Spencer opened the fridge and took out a pitcher of sweet tea. He put four glasses and the tea on the table, then rummaged through the pantry and found a box of Moon Pies. They were just finishing their chocolate-marshmallow treats when Spencer's mom came in the kitchen.

"What's with the different colored ribbons, Mom? The only time you've ever added another color is when you brought us home from the hospital. You're not having another baby, are you?" Spencer joked.

"Heavens no," she said. "But we are having some special visitors for dinner tonight."

"Really?" Spencer asked. "Who's special enough to warrant ribbons on the willow?"

"Oh," Mrs. Wilson said nonchalantly, "just the president and his wife."

"The president of what?" asked Claire, assuming it was maybe the president of Mr. Wilson's software development company.

"The United States of America," Mrs. Wilson

said with a smile so proud you could practically see the American flag waving in the glint of her eyes. She gathered everyone together to fill them in on the details of the presidential visit.

As was well known among the American people, the first lady of the United States had announced her massive anti-bullying initiative earlier in the year. Before her husband took office, she had served as a public school teacher. Preventing bullying had always been a major concern of hers.

Through training and educational campaigns, her task force had made many inroads. But the impact that the Benton Birdies had made in a just a few short weeks was unprecedented. When she told her husband that she wanted to go to North Carolina to meet the children who had started it all, he thought it was a splendid idea and decided to make the trip with her. The White House staff jumped into action arranging all the details to make this visit happen.

"Why didn't you tell us when you first found out?" asked Abby.

"I thought I'd let Willodean tell you," she responded. They all turned to look out the window at the ribbons on the willow.

"She sure knows how to keep a secret," Spencer said. "We walked right past her and her red, white, and blue ribbons, and she didn't say a mumbling word."

"Well she should have told you not to make a

mess in here," his mom said, looking at the Moon Pie wrappers and chocolate crumbs scattered all over the kitchen table. "Quick, clean this up! The president is coming over for dinner!"

CHAPTER THIRTY-EIGHT

Something Very Special to Celebrate

THE PRESIDENTIAL VISIT WAS a once-in-a-lifetime thing that none of the people at the dinner could ever have imagined happening. Mrs. Wilson was a nervous wreck leading up to the event. It was challenging enough hosting eighteen people for dinner, but it took it to a whole new level when the president of the United States and the first lady were among the guests!

What came as some relief to Spencer's mom was that the White House arranged to have the fully prepared meal, dessert, and coffee delivered and served by a culinary team from the president's staff. The staff even set up two additional tables in the living room to accommodate the Champion, Boylan, and McCalister parents, Grandpa Theodore, and all the siblings. Spencer, Claire, Jeremy, Sheila, Mr. and Mrs. Wilson, and the president and first lady would be seated in the dining room.

* * *

"What a warm welcome," the president said after the official introductions were made. "Those ribbons on the tree. Very nice."

"Oh," Rudy said, "you saw the ribbons on Willodean, Mr. President?"

"Willodean?" the president asked.

Spencer then explained the tradition of the ribbon on the willow to the president and his wife.

"That's lovely," said the first lady to Mrs. Wilson, "What a beautiful tradition."

"Yeah," said Rudy, "but it's only when there's something *very* special to celebrate. Like you coming to visit! That's why they're there."

"Only when there's something *very* special to celebrate," the first lady said like she was learning top secret, critical information. "Got it."

After dinner as the group sat in the living room having dessert, tea, and coffee, the first lady talked at length with the kids about their initiative and about its impact. She was impressed with the power of the countless comments attached to the now viral video.

"I hope you never give up bringing awareness to this cause," she told them. "You could also use your platform to spread the importance of not being a silent bystander to bullying."

"Yes ma'am," the kids responded.

The conversation then turned to other things that the kids were interested in, and ultimately came back around to badminton.

"So why badminton, Spencer?" asked the president. "What got you interested in that game?"

Spencer explained about the set that he had received when he was eight and that he and Claire had been playing since that time.

"I hear you're pretty good," said the president.

"We enjoy playing," Spencer said.

"I'd love to see you in action. How about we go out back, and you teach us how it's done. The first lady and I against you and Claire."

Spencer, in his wildest imagination, could have never envisioned playing a game of badminton against the president of the United States. He was almost speechless.

"Ah..." he stammered as he looked to Claire for a nod, "Yes, Mr. President, we'd be honored."

* * *

"Now, don't go easy on us, you two," the president said when they were situated on either side of the net.

"Oh, we won't, sir," Spencer said as the fans on the sidelines—Jeremy, Sheila, the parents, all the siblings, and four Secret Service agents in dark suits—chuckled. Boots, naturally, was there and smiling too.

About halfway through the game Spencer gave a coach's time out signal. "We can't have all the fun here. I'm thinking it's time to send our other players in to finish the match." He used his racket to beckon Jeremy and Sheila to replace them on the court.

"No," Jeremy and Sheila said together. Then Jeremy said, "Thanks, Spence, but y'all got this. Carry on, my friends."

They finished the second half just as the sun was starting to set. By order of the president, Spencer and Claire didn't go easy on their opponents. The final score was 21-1. After game point, the players shook hands and congratulated each other on a fine match.

Boots lead the way as the group walked back into the house. After a round of thank yous and goodbyes, the president and his wife walked to the waiting limousine. As they came to Willodean, the first lady stopped and gazed for a moment at the ribbons. She looked back at Rudy, who was standing on the walk with the others.

"Only when there's something *very* special to celebrate, right?" she asked.

"Yes ma'am," Rudy said, raising his hand to wave goodbye.

Something Very Special to Celebrate • 193

As the motorcade pulled away, the group watched the red taillights fade as the cars made their way down Cardinal Lane.

* * *

A few weeks later the telephone rang while Mrs. Wilson was making supper.

"Wilson residence," she answered.

"Hold for the President of the United States please," a voice said.

Mrs. Wilson quickly put her hand over the receiver and called her family into the kitchen, "It's the president," she whispered as she hit the speaker button so all could hear.

"Mrs. Wilson," came the friendly voice of the president, "I hope you and your family are doing well. The first lady wanted me to personally call you and tell you that there will be a televised ceremony in the Rose Garden tomorrow at two p.m. She and her task force will be announcing their new anti-bullying initiative and releasing a set of official guidelines that schools can use to combat the problem. I'll also be announcing some funding sources that will be made available to the schools to help carry out the guidelines. We hope that all of you there can tune in."

"We wouldn't miss it, sir. Thank you for calling, and please thank the first lady for thinking of us."

They both said their goodbyes, and Mrs.

Wilson carefully placed the phone back in its dock.

"Well, I'll be darned," Grandpa Theodore said. And the rest of the Wilsons just smiled at the thought of what had happened. The president of the United States had just called their home.

* * *

The next afternoon the whole group gathered at the Wilson home to watch the Rose Garden ceremony. Spencer's mom made a blackberry cobbler to serve with the homemade ice cream that his dad made in the rock salt ice cream freezer.

The program started with a closeup shot of a reporter announcing the upcoming ceremony. "Here come the president and the first lady now," the reporter said as the camera panned out to include them in the frame.

Rudy noticed it first. "Look!" he said as the rest of the group's eyes followed where he was pointing. There, behind the first lady who was standing at the podium, they saw a large tree. Around its trunk was a wide red ribbon, tails fluttering in the breeze.

The first lady said, "We are gathered here today because we have something *very* special to celebrate."

The group listened to her explain the details of the anti-bullying initiative and to the president as he discussed the funding for this new program.

Although the camera was focused on the

speakers at the podium, the group from Benton, North Carolina, kept their eyes on the tree with the red ribbon in corner of the screen.

After the ceremony was over and the cameras cut back to the reporter, Spencer got up and headed toward the front door. As he passed the cabinet where his mom kept her red ribbons, he grabbed one off the top shelf. His three friends followed and helped him as he tied the ribbon around the willow.

"A better world. That's what the ribbon means today," he said. "And that is something *very* special to celebrate."

The four stood back to look at the ribbon on the willow and smiled broadly. The sun that shone through the wispy leaves made it seem as if the tree itself was smiling back at them.

About the Author

Jody Cleven lives with her husband and her golden retriever in a log cabin surrounded by Carolina pines. After years of teaching kids, teaching adults to teach kids, and raising three kids of her own, she's seen it all when it comes to kids' drama, fears, hopes, and dreams. It's those experiences that inform the heart-warming and hope-filled stories she writes to inspire and entertain kids of all ages. The majority of her career was spent in the field of education as a teacher, assistant principal, and university professor. She is also the author of *A Ripple in Maggie Pond*. Ask any student she's ever had, and they'll tell you her three favorite words in the universe are "Read, read, read."